Advanced Praise for *In the Wake of the Willows*

"Mr. Thurber should be ashamed of himself for such a scurrilous and contemptible depiction of my dear grandfather, Mr. Toad."

ℰ Baroness Raquel Toad, Westport Point, Massachusetts

"You are sure to see this book in the newspapers, literally,… after it has been pulped and turned into newsprint." *ℰ The Tidewater Beacon*

"A squid could have inked a better book, and it would have smelled a whole lot better."

ℰ Haggis McBadger

"The author of this book should be condemned for promoting and glorifying the scandalous sport of croquet. This book can only serve to promote the moral decay of our community." *ℰ Rev. Cotton Mather III*

"Mr. Thurber: You might have imagined your libelous depiction of my client's family to be amusing, but my client did not. You repeated the outrageous and discredited claim that his weasel relatives had been convicted of overdue library books, but there are no records for this baseless and defamatory claim, never mind their other heinous crimes such as mismatched socks, jay walking, split infinitives, bad breath, and appalling table manners. See you in court!" *ℰ Crassus "Buddy" Weasel III, Esq.*

"Lies, lies, damnable lies." *ℰ Portly Otter III*

"Since I am a literary agent, my job is to reject manuscripts, thousands and thousands of them. These submissions quickly become a blur, but Mr. Thurber's manuscript was so painfully bad that it stood out from the slush pile. It was with immense pleasure that I sent him a tart rejection letter. Imagine my shock and horror when I found this abomination at a local book store." *ℰ Noelle A. Vail, Sisyphus Literary Agency*

"Upon reading this book, I felt betrayed. After we had extracted a solemn promise from Mr. Thurber to protect our privacy, he gleefully penned a tawdry exposé. His scurrilous and mendacious interpretation of our history has made a mockery of our community."

ℰ Marten Fisher, The Riverside Historical Society

In the Wake of the Willows

A Sequel to Kenneth Grahame's
The Wind in the Willows

by
Frederick Gorham Thurber

Illustrated by
Amy Thurber

Cricket Works Press
South Dartmouth, MA

Cricket Works Press
South Dartmouth, MA 02748

Distributed to the trade by Willows.link

Library of Congress Control Number:2019906274

Library of Congress Cataloging-in-Publication Data

Names: Thurber, Frederick Gorham, author. | Thurber, Amy, illustrator.
Title: In the Wake of the Willows: A Sequel to Kenneth Grahame's The Wind in the Willows
/ by Frederick Gorham Thurber ; Cover, and interior illustrations by Amy Thurber.
Description: First edition. | South Dartmouth : Cricket Works Press, [2019]
Identifiers: LCCN 2019906274 | ISBN 978-0-578-51287-7 (hardcover)
Subjects: Adventure-Natural History-Humor-Romance-Fiction.
Subjects: LCSH: Animals--Fiction | Friendship--Fiction | River Life--Fiction | Boating--Fiction |
BISAC: FICTION / Classics. | FICTION / Fairy Tales, Folk Tales, Legends & Mythology. |
FICTION / Historical.

Printed in the United States of America on 50# creme paper

Willows.link

First edition 1 2 3 4 5 6 7 8 9

Book design by Amy Thurber

Text set in Adobe Goudy. Titles set in Bernhard Modern.

CRICKET
WORKS
PRESS

Contents

The Beetle

To my wife for motivating me to write this book.
She said that since I resemble Mr. Toad in so many ways,
that I might as well write about him. ℰ FGT

To my dear husband for being patient,
while these illustrations traveled the world,
and came back to him. ℰ AT

Disclaimer

I am sure that you are weary of the usual disclaimers in a book such as this, but I am here to say that all the characters in this book are based on real animals. Any resemblance to humans or contemporary organizations is strictly coincidental, except for the unfortunate parallels between Mr. Toad and the author. The events that I describe, while seemingly fantastic, are all backed up by contemporaneous accounts that The Riverside Historical Society has in their files. It is easy to dismiss some of these extraordinary claims, but to this day artifacts of these remarkable events can still be found in Toad Hall, along The River, at The Inn, and even as far away as the summit of Nanda Devi in the Himalaya Mountains.

Author's Preface

While in dry dock during a recent convalescence, I had occasion to re-read *The Wind in the Willows*. In doing so, I had to wonder, as I had so many times before, why the story of our local, New World animals had never been told. I have always felt that these fellows were equally as interesting and compelling as their cousins across the sea.

Coverage of the local River history has been sporadic at best. The reader may well be aware of the lively dust up between our local Mr. Toad and the Norwegian polar explorer, Roald Amundsen, the unfortunate war of words between Mr. Rat and the British birding journals of the day, the scholarly discussions of the *Ode to Toad*, or even Mr. Toad's extraordinary conquest in the Himalayas, but this is only part of the story. This book is an attempt to fill in the gaps and tell the full story that occurred one fateful summer almost a century ago.

I am motivated to record this local lore while there are still residents of The River who know of these remarkable events. During my research on this subject, I discovered that the history was far richer than I had supposed, and I am pleased to share this history with you, dear reader.

Introduction

This is a story about the denizens of a very special New World river. For like their relatives on the other side of the Ocean, this river had its own Rat, Mole, Badger, Otter, and Weasel clans. Although some arrived thanks to famine and other crises, most could trace their lineage back to their bold ancestors who traveled with other pilgrims on the *Mayflower* to seek their freedom and fortune in the New World.

How the Weasels got here is not clear for there is no record of them on the Mayflower's manifest, or in other passenger lists that I could find. The consensus is that they were asked, in no uncertain terms, to leave a corsair that was watering at Tarpaulin Cove because their uncouth behavior and bad manners had so offended the pirates manning this vessel.

Although it is not clear how the Weasels arrived at The River, they certainly cut a wide swath when here. I was able to track their progress from police blotters, investigations of the vice squad, records from the game wardens, citations by the harbormaster, and the ship's logs of the local revenue cutters pursuing rumrunners. Through the centuries, the weasels were known for various criminal activities such as overdue library books, mismatched socks, split infinitives, appalling posture, jay-walking, underhanded croquet play, terrible dental hygiene, and, worst of all, very poor manners.

Here in New England the transplants from the Old Country, both good and not so good, found their own River, comfortable and familiar, but close enough to the sea so that its waters mingled with the salt. For generation after generation they lived here, befriending the native animals and putting down deep roots. You probably know quite a bit about their cousins on their native Thames, but I hope you will also enjoy reading about the other Mr. Toad and his friends.

Frederick Gorham Thurber

❖ Part 1 ❖
The Nocturnal Terror

❖ Chapter 1 ❖

A Monster Haunts the Riverfront

> "Always, when the surface is calm enough and the light is favorable, the river seems shot through and through with tremblings and premonitions... One secret of success in observing Nature is capacity to take a hint... It is not so much what we see as what the thing seen suggests. "
> ∫ John Burroughs, Signs and Seasons, 1886

If not for the newly arrived Monster, this season would have started like so many others along The River.

It had been a typical off-season along the riverbank. Through the snows, frosts and winter's other indignities, nature's seeds had rested underground, their faint embers of life patiently waiting for that fine spring day when a warm southwest wind off the ocean would fan them to life. That day came in mid-April this year when Aeolus summoned the sea wind to drive off winter's icy shackles. From every branch and patch of ground, green tendrils reached for the sun as the land awoke.

Across the community there was a bustle and buzz of preparation for what promised to be another delightful summer. Gardens were weeded, burrows swept out, fences painted, and windows washed. Nests were built, holes excavated, and dens lined. The trees had begun to leaf out, and the songbirds had arrived to glean their foliage. Every morning more and more voices joined the chorus as new arrivals tried to get in a few words to announce the day until it was a joyous dawn cacophony of birdsong.

The nautical set was also busy getting ready. Mr. Rat's catboat, the *Beetle*, had been launched and was happily bobbing at her slip, shimmering under a fresh coat of varnish, tugging at her traces, and eager to be off. Mr. and Mrs. Badger had moved out of their subterranean winter quarters in the Wild Wood to their 41-foot yawl, *The Concordia*, which was tied up at the long wharf. The farmers had just planted their summer corn, and their peas were already setting flowers. Mrs. Badger's roses had been pruned and were putting out new shoots. Everything pointed to another fine season along The River, or so it seemed.

But there was a problem; the first inkling of the coming crisis was already upon them. The River was in a strange mood this year; something was just not right. A new creature had moved in along the waterfront and begun a terrifying caterwauling and thwacking at night. The local folk were quite alarmed; The River was a tranquil place and nothing like this had been heard before. Sounds carry a long way on the water, and everyone had an opinion about the source. It was not Beaver and his chainsaw; the locals knew that unpleasant sound all too well. This terrible shrieking appeared to come from a distressed, or at least highly animated, creature.

Mr. Rat was convinced it was a Loon. As he explained, the indigenous Cree believed the Loon's call was the lament of a fallen warrior denied access to heaven. Many of the other children in the riverfront community favored this theory, but Mr. Rat's daughter, Rickie, did not. Rickie was the local authority on birds and thought the terrible sounds were something far more sinister.

Investigating the shore one morning, Rickie was alarmed to find clumps of marsh grass that looked like they had been torn from the mud flats and chewed up. Some titanic struggle was unfolding at night on The River. Was it tooth and claw and flying fur? Maybe, but Rickie had her doubts.

Some said the howling was a hobo bobcat coming to visit, others said it was the barn owls that had recently been discovered in a silo at the Tripp farm. There were even some tall "tails" about roosters, but these were quickly dismissed. The superstitious among the river folk started to tell spooky stories about a Banshee they saw at night that had come to foretell a death in the community.

No one was quite sure what the source of the noise was, but the consensus seemed to be that an Eastern Mountain Lion, also known as a Catamount, had moved in; nothing else could wail so dreadfully. Several sources claimed to have even seen the big cat quietly padding along the riverbank, its long, thick tail twitching and swishing. One witness drew a sketch of it, which was put on warning posters around town. After dinner, activities were canceled, and the riverfront community started locking their doors at night (something that they had never done before). Pit traps were dug for the Catamount, but all they caught was a groggy Mr. Toad wobbling back from The Inn late one night, much to the annoyance of a skunk that was also in the trap.

A dangerous beast was on the loose, and the community was on edge. Parents were now nervously escorting their children to and from school. The constable hired extra deputies to help guard the community and reassure its inhabitants. Why the Catamount had moved in, and what it was dining on, was a source of much speculation and worry.

Another problem that vexed the placid waters of The River was the ocean swells. Old Neptune, it would seem, was sending feelers far up River, jiggling the wine glasses at Boathouse row and rocking the yachts at their moorings. Even Badger, snug in the cabin of his splendid yawl, the Concordia, noticed the tea sloshing in his cup. One night The River ran over its banks, and the salt burned Mrs. Badger's riverside rose garden. It was assumed that the winter storms had rearranged the bottom in such a way that the ocean could now get into their quiet anchorage, but no one could say for sure.

There were other troubles along The River, as well. The locals along the waterfront were puzzled by the mysterious channels that began appearing in the salt marshes and sandbars along the bends and oxbows of The River. Some thought that this was related to the ocean swells that were running up The River. Most assumed that the meandering River had changed its mind about the best route to the sea, as it is wont to do, and was feeling out a new passage. Some boaters were grateful for the shortcuts, but the inquisitive Rickie was puzzled. Why were these channels in a neat line? It was not like The River to come straight to the point; it preferred to tell its tale in a meandering, roundabout sort of way. Rickie tried to dismiss her ponderings on this subject, but once an idea fetched up in her mind, she could never shake it until she had seen it through to resolution.

Everyone could sense that there was something off-kilter along The River, but few could articulate their doubts. The Ospreys were unusually irritable this spring, scolding and screeching and shooing all visitors away and altogether being very unsociable. The eider ducks and cormorants were jittery and scattered when approached. The clamming was slow and few scallops were seen castanet-ing around the shallows. Even the flounder and striped bass seemed hesitant to enter their usual haunts on the sand bars and reefs of The River.

There is a balance and harmony to The River as it revolves through the seasons. When The River is out of balance, the residents can feel it, and this year there was a palpable sense of unease and apprehension about the approaching summer.

The unthinkable was starting to happen. Some residents started to whisper that their companion and provider, The River, reliable friend to countless generations, was no longer a safe anchorage.

Although there was a great deal of concern about the coming season, no one could have anticipated the scope of the coming crisis, nor could anyone imagine that the fate of the riverfront and even the lives of some of its inhabitants would depend on the actions of the most irresponsible member of the community. In the months to follow, the smallest detail such as the twist of a knot, a voice in the wind, the turn of the tide, or the wing of a curlew, would have the most profound consequences and the greatest responsibility would be borne by the least qualified.

For this was but the first inkling of the drama to come…

❖ Chapter 2 ❖
The Catamount Captured

"They growl and suddenly caterwaul into falsetto--the famous scarifying, metallic scream functioning as a kind of hunting cry close up, to terrorize and start the game."

    ƒ Edward Hoagland, "Hailing the Elusory Mountain Lion",
    Walking the Dead Diamond River

"In the daytime the cougar is seldom seen, but its peculiar cry frequently thrills the experienced traveler with horror."

    ƒ John D. Godman, *American Natural History*, 1826

"Rickie," said Mr. Rat, waking his daughter. "It would be a fine day for a shakedown cruise and a chance to scout the dunes for beach plums."

So began Rat and Rickie's eventful first outing of the season. Any unsettling thoughts about The River's strange mood was far from their minds as they prepared for a trip to the dunes behind the beach. Ostensibly the goal was to scout for blooming beach plums, but they both knew it was just an excuse to get out in the boat after a long winter. It would have been much less "trouble" to cross the bridge by carriage and walk to the dunes, but in this case, as in most other cases, the trip itself was more important than the actual destination. As everyone in the community knew, days spent on The River were the only ones that really counted.

The first excursion of the year was always memorable, but as they set out this day, they had no idea just how eventful it would be.

There was a gentle breeze freshening from the southwest as Mr. Rat and his daughter boarded their sturdy little catboat, the *Beetle*, and headed for a sheltered cove where they could beach their shallow draft boat. It was a bright cheerful day, the first Perfect Day of the year, and full of the promise of many such days to come.

They slipped their lines, headed for the channel, and then tacked downriver on the falling tide with a tip of the cap to old friends who were also out enjoying this splendid day.

It was Rickie's trick at the helm as Mr. Rat coached his daughter on the finer points of tacking upwind.

"That's it, point her a little higher. See how much she will bear," advised Rickie's patient teacher.

Down The River they went, thoroughly enjoying this sparkling day on the water.

"Watch the luff. She is spilling her wind. Ease off a point or so," said Mr. Rat as he showed his daughter how to get the most out of the catboat.

As they worked downriver, Rickie noticed that some of the cork channel markers were looking rather bedraggled, while other buoys did not appear to be set out at all. This would simply not do; with the boating season about to start, the Harbormaster needed to have the byways clearly marked. Rickie asked her father to talk to the Harbormaster about it later that day.

As they sailed close to a ragged channel marker, Rickie pointed it out to her father.

"Say, Dad, this buoy looks like something has taken a bite out of it."

"I don't see any teeth marks."

"It looks like something with a beak took a chunk out of it. Could this be the monster making all that noise at night?"

"The only thing with a beak that big is a sea turtle such as a Leatherback. Leatherbacks eat jellyfish, though they sometimes mistake lobster buoys for jellyfish and get tangled in the lines."

"Jellyfish? Ick! I would rather eat a channel marker."

"Leatherbacks do not come into The River, and they do not howl."

"Maybe the monster is not a reptile like the Leatherback turtle at all. Hmmm, could it be an amphibian?"

13

"Who ever heard of a howling frog?"

Mr. Rat and his daughter left the channel marker and set a course, close hauled on the starboard tack, for the backside of the barrier beach. The Ocean glinted in the bright May sunlight as they approached the shore.

Acting Captain Rickie put the *Beetle's* head up into the wind while acting First Mate Mr. Rat raised the centerboard. The sail, indecisive in the face of the wind, shilly-shallied about from starboard to larboard in noisy white ripples. Then the *Beetle's* forefoot made a satisfying scrunch as it ran up on the sand, buffing up its new coat of copper paint.

Mr. Rat ran the anchor up the beach with Rickie keeping it taut. Then he tossed the auxiliary anchor off the stern and kedged the *Beetle* out a bit so she would not be left high and dry on the dropping tide. Next the halyards were loosened and the sail brought down, clattering on its hoops, and wrapped up in its gaskets to stop any mischievous tricks by the wind. With everything secure and ship shape, father and daughter set out along a sandy path in the dunes. The air was redolent with the scent of sweet fern and flowering beach rose as they wended their way along the trail.

First stop was the highest dune, which the local youngsters nicknamed Spyglass Hill, to reconnoiter. Every year Rat was in friendly competition with Fox for the biggest beach plum haul. This year they were determined to find some secret plum bushes securely hidden from the avaricious Fox. As they poked here and there, taking notes and drawing maps, the masked bandit faces of the Yellowthroat Warblers that darted through the briars reminded them of their rival. Prairie Warblers serenaded them with their ascending notes and bank swallows zipped around them snapping their bills and picking off bugs. Along the way Rickie harvested beach rose blossoms for Mrs. Badger's candied rose-petal garnish.

The scouting and mapping was rewarding and the picnic even more so, but before they could set sail home, the southwest wind had faltered and the sun had begun to set. When the warm moist air from the land met the cool ocean air, there was a tug of war for the moisture; their compromise was fog, which started to send its tendrils snaking over and around the dunes to ensnare the little animals. Rat and Rickie's world started to contract as the lights from river houses across the way winked out in a white blanket and then the sand bar and finally the dunes were gone. This envelope snuffed out the voices from across the river and muffled the beating of the surf. Their world had been reduced to a shimmering sphere only a few rods wide.

On The Ocean such a fog would be a deadly situation, but they were on the friendly River, and one of them was an experienced helmsman, so what could have been a dangerous situation became an enjoyable adventure. Ratty calmly lit the stern light, and they cast off into the flood tide, with Rickie in the bow casting the lead and calling off the depth.

Rat manned the tiller, watched the water, and glanced at the compass now and then. He calmly steered the little catboat out to the channel, careful to avoid the submerged breakwater that had been the undoing of so many other craft. Mr. Rat knew these waters well and understood how each stage of the tide changed their appearance so he could read the ripples, currents, glassy humps, and minor eddies & boils to navigate the channel. Rat could even distinguish the tangy, salty smell of The Ocean water from the fecund eelgrass, clam-mud smells of The River.

The only sounds were the rattling of the hoops on the mast, the gentle slap of slippered wavelets against the cedar planking, the plunk of the sounding lead, and the gently foaming gurgle that the rudder left in their wake. Rickie was startled by a sudden pop, but Mr. Rat explained that it was a small Striped Bass splashing under some minnows. It was just another workday underwater, for the fishy denizens of The River were going about their business unconcerned with the minor drama that was about to unfold on the surface.

As Rat and Rickie worked their way upriver, their damp clothes clung to their fur like a cold blanket, and fog droplets dripped from their eyelashes causing them to blink as they tried to peer through the murk. They looked down into the clear limpid water of The River, watching the bottom silently glide by, and admired the phosphorescent Comb Jellies that indignantly lit up in response to the sounding lead intruding into their watery world.

With their senses sharpened by the fog and the tricky navigation, the two animals were on the alert. After rounding the sand bar at the entrance of The River, they began the reach back to their slip. The ever-observant Rickie noticed something different. On most days, neither would have seen it, but now they were mindful for any sign of trouble.

"Dad, take a look at this. There is an oil slick on the water. What could cause that?"

"I am not sure Rickie, but I wouldn't worry about it."

"It smells disgusting; something is not right."

As they worked their way home, Rickie saw something else that started to concern her.

"Dad, the water right here near the marsh is gray. Why isn't it clear like the rest of The River? I don't like it; it seems suspicious."

"Rickie, I am sure it is nothing. Maybe Otter was out clamming today and stirred up the bottom. Let's get home before we catch a chill."

But Rickie would have none of it. There was something wrong, something peculiar, something out of place with her River. After much cajoling, she convinced her father to come about and follow the muddy stream of water. Mr. Rat was used to his daughter's incessant curiosity, but he was getting cold and his stomach was rumbling.

However as Mr. Rat peered into the river he too could see the stream of muddy water, and it was getting more concentrated; they must be approaching its source. But there was more. As the two animals looked closely, they saw chewed up pieces of marsh grass, bits of pulverized clam shells, and, a stream of bubbles roiling up from the bottom. Nope, this was not right, not right at all. Mr. Rat's hackles were up and his anxiety level was rising. He expertly followed the stream of detritus until it led right up onto the marsh following a fresh channel that had just been carved through the mud and marl.

"Just as I suspected. It is him. That pesky twerp," declared Rickie.

"Who do you mean?" asked her Dad.

"Follow the channel, Dad. You are not going to like what you find," said Rickie, and she was right.

The resident Osprey screeched as Rat nosed the catboat into the channel. By careful maneuvering, and with Rickie in the bow fending off with the boat hook, Rat was able to wiggle the *Beetle* through this unfamiliar byway in the marsh. As they advanced, they could hear a rumbling and growling and coughing. The air was full of an acrid burning smell. Then they heard a grinding of metal and a whine, and finally a screeching gasp and clunk as whatever it was seized up and expired. At last Rat and Rickie came to the end of the channel and found it plugged by an enormous boxy presence, dark and menacing in the moonlight. A furious Rat realized what it was and glowered at the monstrosity. Rickie, too, scowled at this apparition, which was still shaking and smoking.

As the delicate catboat approached this hulk, Rat could make out the name

"*Runabout*" on the transom of the beast. He hailed the craft and up popped the familiar face of Mr. Toad's son, Toady.

"Oh Hi there, just in time. I appear to be a bit stuck. Is this a new reef? I don't remember it? Throw me a line there, and tow me out, if you will."

For a long while, a grim Mr. Rat just stared at Toady.

"Toady, my boy," explained a stern Mr. Rat. "This will not do. The fog is thickening and the moon will soon set; we will have to wait for the Launch to pull you off on tomorrow's flood. You have to come back with us. Right Now!"

"Shan't," replied a defiant Toady.

"You SHALL," responded Mr. Rat. "Strike your colors and come aboard the *Beetle*."

Toady was desperate. This was his father's gleaming new mahogany speedboat, the *Runabout*. Rickie could see its mud-spattered brightwork and polished brass shimmering in the moonlight. As both Mr. Rat and Toady knew full well, the youngster was not supposed to take the *Runabout* out on his own. And he was definitely not supposed to take it out at night. And he was absolutely, positively not supposed to use it for running down channel markers at high speed, or gouging new channels in the marsh, or creating huge wakes in The River, or spewing out rooster tails of tortured water behind the boat.

Speedboats were new to the River. Mr. Rat had occasionally seen Mr. Toad out with young Toady sedately chuffing up and down the waterways, just puttering along, visiting old friends and taking outings to the beach and generally being a solid citizen on the water. The River folk were used to the slow, gentle rumblings of the *Runabout's* engine, but had never heard anything like the scream of its 12 cylinders at full throttle.

Old Toad had calmed down after resolving his various legal and financial troubles. He was now a proper, respectable Toad, as all his friends had known he would become. Most of Mr. Toad's time these days, when not on the water, was spent telling colorful stories at The Inn. On many nights, with a sly twinkle in his eye, Mr. Toad would tell tall tales of dubious veracity about the daring exploits of his youth to wide-eyed newcomers at The Inn.

In any case, with considerable urging, Rat convinced a despondent and ashen-faced Toad Junior that the jig was up and his night was over. He could not stay in the *Runabout* all night and must come back with them. He reluctantly furled his flag and hopped aboard the *Beetle*.

After sailing up to the slip and securing the *Beetle*, Rat, Rickie and a reluctant Toady, set off for Toad Hall. Mr. Toad was not home and the crestfallen young Toady moped into the great house, but before he did, Rickie thought of something so obvious that she was worried that Toady would be insulted if she asked. But it had to be asked, so she came right out with it.

"So Toady, ahem, I assume you set the anchor before leaving the *Runabout*, right?"

"Anchor? What anchor?" asked Toady in puzzlement.

"Toady!!!" scolded Rickie.

"What's the big deal with the anchor," asked Toady.

"The anchor is the most important piece of safety gear on a boat," said Rickie.

"How so?"

"What's the tide doing, Toady?" responded Rickie.

"I dunno. Why does it matter?"

"It is incoming. And what happens when the tide comes in?"

"The water level rises…oh wait, oh my, goodness, gosh…oh dear," The puzzlement drained from Toady's face to be replaced by recognition and then deep despair and panic as he realized what this meant. So began Toady's "complex" relationship with anchors.

"We must go back immediately. I insist!" cried the desperate young Toad.

"I am afraid that will not be possible," sighed an exasperated Mr. Rat. "The moon has set and the fog has thickened. It is time to stand down for the night. Head to bed, and we will deal with it in the morning."

So the *Runabout's* wanderings this day were not yet over. Sometime that night, their friend, The River, would gently lift the *Runabout* from the marsh and bring it along on its meandering journeys, pulled by the moon this way and that.

Mr. Rat dreaded the unpleasant task of informing Old Mr. Toad, but first a little background on his son, Toady.

Chapter 3

The Two Little Terrors

"We think boys are rude, insensitive animals but it is not so in all cases.
Each boy has one or two sensitive spots…"
ℰ Mark Twain, My Autobiography, 1909

Mr. Toad's son, Toady, had a bit of a reputation in town, nothing serious, but the consensus was that the apple had not fallen far from the tree. He and Mr. Otter's son, Portly, were quite the mischievous pair, and the two of them were always looking for trouble. Luckily for everyone concerned, real trouble was rather hard to find along The River. Sure, the boys would get peppered by hornet stings, or get stuck in briars, or their campfire in the dunes might get out of control, or they might be chased by a farmer for stealing apples, but these incidents were not unusual for Riverside children.

More serious were the pranks instigated by Toady and Portly. Whenever a snake was discovered in a girl's lunch bag, or fermented mackerel ended up in the local mailboxes, or a neighbor's cat was sporting extra stripes, or sandpaper ended up in the toilet paper rolls, or peanut butter & jellyfish sandwiches mysteriously showed up at the church social, or an eel was found swimming in the water cooler at school, the authorities would sigh and say, "Round up the usual suspects." By "usual suspects" they meant young Toady and Portly.

The two did not hold up very well to interrogation, and in short order the truth would be uncovered and punishment meted out.

The two little devils were not so careful about covering up their crimes. One incident that showed their lack of guile was when the redoubtable Mrs. Badger found dirty, webbed tracks, reeking of clam mud, leading in her door, through the living room, across her Moroccan carpet, into the kitchen, and right to the cookie jar. Toady was surprised when he was apprehended for this caper.

When two shark fins that looked suspiciously like doctored up snorkels were seen patrolling off the beach, terrifying the swimmers, the authorities quickly apprehended the culprits before Mr. Otter got out his harpoon.

Punishment usually fit the crime Toady and Portly spent many perfectly beautiful days, those that could have been better spend swimming, fishing, teasing other children, and generally goofing around, on washing carpets, scrubbing floors, de-scenting mailboxes, bathing cats (a tricky business, that), and worst of all, working at the church socials.

One punishment that the chortling Weasel children particularly enjoyed was when Toady and Portly, after the Mackerel Caper, were put on manure duty. The powers that be thought they needed a smelly lesson. First Toady and Portly had to visit the Silas farm and muck out the stalls, Augean Stables, as it seemed to them. Then they were stationed on Silas' manure-spreader wagon as the farmer hitched up his bray and set out. The two hardened criminals rode around on the wagon and shoveled the manure onto the fields.

The Weasel children were not the only ones who enjoyed watching Toady and Portly spreading manure. While Barn Swallows may swoop and soar and dive, doing their farm chores of cleaning up bugs, the Mockingbirds, those lazy miscreants, like to hang about and cause trouble. Those nagging Mockingbirds had a great time gliding by, flashing their wings and scolding the two boys. One particular Mockingbird enjoyed repeating his scold three times, as Mockingbirds tend to do, because one taunt was not enough. The boys were treated to an endless series of insults such as:

Naughty, naughty, naughty

Caught'ya, caught'ya, caught'ya

Manure for you, manure for you, manure for you

Dirty boys, dirty boys, dirty boys

Guilty, Guilty, Guilty

And so on all day long.

Toady and Portly gritted their teeth and vowed revenge on their tormentor. Portly suggested caging the pesky bird and bringing him inside so the cat could keep an eye on him. Toady suggested that once he was caged, the perfect job for him would be in a coal mine. Portly thought that they should paint his feathers an embarrassing chartreuse. Toady thought he should be plucked and the feathers used as a duster. Portly suggested even better, the mockingbird should be stuffed and used on one of those ridiculous bird hats that were so popular with the high-society ladies. These plans were all fine and dandy, but the boys could never quite figure out how to get the salt on the tail of that pesky bird.

That night, after being scrubbed, disinfected, washed, and rinsed and washed again, Toady gained admittance to Toad Hall. He headed straight to bed, but was dismayed to hear the Mockingbird, who dearly loved to perform a nocturne, at his window describing their crimes to the Moon:

Toady-Portly, Toady-Portly, Toady-Portly

Manure-men, Manure-men, Manure-men

Big Trouble, Big Trouble, Big Trouble

Grounded, Grounded, Grounded.

The closest that Toady and Portly got to Real Trouble was the infamous Mole Crab Incident. Mole crabs are wiggly creatures the size of jellybeans that burrow in the wet sand at the beach. Young Toady loved to dig them out of the retreating waves and feel them work between his fingers. Mole crabs don't bite or pinch, but they are exceedingly squirmy as they try to burrow to safety.

The Trouble started when the boys discovered how delightful it was to drop some mole crabs down the swimsuits of the young animals at the beach. As they watched, the stricken young animals would run screaming and squirming and hopping down the beach, with their mothers in hot pursuit. Very satisfying, they thought, like lighting off a skyrocket, and great sport. Great sport until they made the grievous mistake of seeding the suit of Mrs. Badger's beloved granddaughter, Millicent ('Mini' for short).

They were having a good laugh and a chortle at their cleverness when they felt the enormous paws of Mr. Badger close on the scruff of their necks. They were lifted up, inches away from his craggy face as Mr. Badger explained, in no uncertain terms, that Mrs. Badger wanted to have a word with them. The two airborne boys were brought wiggling and kicking to an audience with Mrs. Badger.

"Here are the wee beasties," declared Mr. Badger as he dropped the two in front of Mrs. Badger.

This meeting ended The Mole Crab Incident, as it has been called in local River Lore. With their interest in mole crabs abruptly terminated, Toady and Portly had to look around for other amusing diversions.

This was all well and good and pretty typical for summer activities of rambunctious children along The River, but for Serious Trouble, one needed a boat. Serious but not dangerous for there was always someone on The River to fish you out of the drink, help you bail out a flooded cockpit, pull you off a sandbar, or help you stand on your centerboard to right your capsized sailboat.

Sailboat trouble was pretty common, even Serious Sailboat Trouble. But, as the town was finding out, for Real Serious Trouble you need a powerboat. Toady was in Real Serious Trouble, the worst of his short life, at least so far.

With the source of all the trouble on The River finally identified, poor Toady's reputation slid from somewhat doubtful to positively horrid after that terrible night. For weeks thereafter the townsfolk shot him disapproving looks and shooed their children away from such a bad apple.

However not all the creatures in the community disapproved; the Weasel children looked upon Toady with new respect and admiration.

❖ Chapter 4 ❖
The Hard Tack

"Have you heard the blinking toad
Sing his solo by the river
When April nights are soft and warm,
And spring is all a-quiver?
If there are jewels in his head,
His wits they often muddle..."
　　　　ℰ John Burroughs, "The Song of the Toad", 1902

Click-clop, click-clop, click-clop went Mr. Rat's shoes on the damp road as he hurried to The Inn. Mr. Toad was sure to be there telling outlandish stories, and Mr. Rat needed to reach him ahead of the bad news. Rumors traveled fast in this small community, and they were due to reach The Inn in short order.

The lamplighters had preceded Mr. Rat, and shafts of yellow glowed through the fog. As he approached the Inn, he could hear the clink of glasses and loud huzzahs. *The Old Boy is on his game tonight* thought Mr. Rat, and he was not looking forward to spoiling the fun.

Mr. Toad was a fixture at The Inn. His legal woes were far in the past, and he was actually a kind and generous member of the community when not behind the wheel of an automobile. It was generally accepted that Toad had grown out of his particular problem, but he was seen to occasionally twitch when he saw an unoccupied motorcar idling in The Inn's stable yard. These days Mr. Toad's favorite pastime was entertaining the guests at The Inn with tall tales of the Toad family exploits, going all the way back to Gaius Toad and the Punic Wars; however, most of Mr. Toad's stories were about the glorious exploits of the most famous Toad of them all, Mr. Toad himself.

Situated at the edge of the harbor, The Inn was a mixing spot for the nautical and farming communities. It had a pub on the ground floor, a ship chandlery adjacent to the pub, and charming, simple rooms upstairs for guests. The Inn's walls were lined with ship's models and heroic portraits of various local luminaries in sporting poses, usually on their mounts. In the chandlery was a highly-polished brass field piece, named the Long Tom; after a glass or two, guests were fond of rolling it out on the patio, and firing it off. It was good for a hearty laugh as the windows in town rattled. The Inn also had a large globe that Toad liked to slowly spin and jab a finger at, all the while saying things such as "There I was in a desperate situation…", or "It was here that we ran into trouble…", or "Imagine my surprise when…"

The heavy, weather-beaten oak door creaked open on bog iron hinges as Mr. Rat entered The Inn. His sensitive nose was assailed by the scent of wood smoke and damp fur. As he worked his way through the crowd, he noticed that all the regulars were in attendance. Rat gave Mr. Mole a pat on the shoulder as he walked by, but Mole was too engrossed by Toad's narrative to notice.

Mr. Rat tipped his hat to that old salt, Mr. Otter, who was snorting and guffawing at each of Mr. Toad's nautical malapropisms.

"Say, Rat old sport," said Mr. Otter. "Did you hear the monster tonight on the water? What a racket…"

"Harrumph", was Mr. Rat's only response.

Mrs. Badger who was standing by the fire rolling her eyes at Toad's story, gave Mr. Rat a knowing smile.

A tangle of conspiratorial weasels were also there snickering and carrying on. Mr. Rat glanced at them disapprovingly.

In addition to the usual crowd at The Inn that night, there was a gaggle of newcomers in awe of Mr. Toad's amazing exploits.

"Want a little something to drive out the chill, Mr. Rat" asked the Innkeeper.

"Not tonight Brenda; I will not be long," replied a grim Mr. Rat.

Toad had his captain's outfit on this night, a confusing mix of American, French, and Turkish uniforms with a large rack of naval ribbons on his chest. Some nights his outfit would be a pith helmet, jodhpurs, and highly polished leather riding boots. On other nights it would be his mountaineering gear, or a Canadian Mounties uniform, or a comically large ten-gallon hat, fringed leather chaps, and a six shooter.

"For me," boasted Toad, puffed up to his fullest, "the sound of a full-force gale tearing through the frozen rigging is music to my ears."

Mr. Rat heard a Weasel named Peevish McWeasel snidely turn to his friends and say in a low voice, "Ha. These days the sound of a cork being pulled from a bottle is the only music to Old Toad's ears."

The Weasel's little circle of friends chortled at this wisecrack. Rat did not; he was upset. Rat scowled at the weasel, "Now, now, Toad is our dear friend. Let him have his fun. He seems to have found some new acolytes."

"'Victims' is more like it," snorted Peevish. Rat thought that Peevish was about the wear out his welcome at The Inn and did not expect to see much of him in the future.

Rat was miffed that the Weasels were not showing Mr. Toad the respect he deserved. Once Toad had been a legend; impossible, uncompromising, unrepentant, but a legend. He had been a shining beacon to the wildness in us all. He had also been a bold warrior and a stout animal in a fight. *Toad is a good fellow, open, friendly, enthusiastic and generous to a fault*, thought Rat, *if a bit slow and simple*.

Rat watched Toad pontificating and stabbing at the globe with a chubby finger. Mr. Rat smiled as he saw the old twinkle back in Toad's eye. The fire and spirit still burned bright as he kept his new friends spellbound. *So, okay*, thought Mr. Rat, *maybe the stories were not exactly 100 percent true. Ah, well maybe a little south of that mark, but the raconteur and his audience were having a darn good time and what's the harm in that?*

"There I was in a desperate struggle," said Toad to the crowd.

"Oh dear," murmured a concerned Mr. Mole.

"When rounding The Horn we were caught in a terrible gale. The crew was certain we were doomed and threatened mutiny; the captain had to post guards around the rum casks."

"Maybe we should do that at The Inn when Toad arrives," whispered

Peevish.

"The barometer was at 27 and falling. The frigid wind was freshening from the south. Mountainous seas threatened to swallow the ship. When we were in a trough, we could barely see the sky and the sails flapped uselessly in the dead air. Then as we were lifted to the foaming crest of a wave, the wind exploded into the sails, giving a report like a thunderclap; you could feel the ship's timbers jolt and hum with the strain of it. Then the ship skidded down the face of the wave into the next trough, and so on through that terrible night.

"The pumps were working continuously but could not keep up, and water was filling the bilge. The royals were sprung and the mizzen was carried away. The night was black as pitch; the only illumination were bolts of lightning slashing across the sky to show a terrible scene of broken spars and tangled cordage. Saint Elmo's fire danced in the rigging as the crew froze in terror. The jolly boat and launch had been smashed; there was no hope of survival if we foundered.

"The captain lost his nerve and retreated to his cabin and his claret. What were we to do? In their darkest hour, the crew turned to me to save them, so I answered the call!

"'Harken to me my boys', I exhorted my crew. 'This is but a sneeze in church after what I have been through.'

"The binnacle was smashed, and I had to use dead reckoning to navigate around The Horn. With sleet lashing my face, and my ship bucking against the strain, I wrestled the lunging wheel as the dark mass of the Horn hove into view. All was certainly lost, thought the crew.

"My confidence never wavered, I'll tell you," continued Toad. "'Now run to the galley,' I ordered the ship's boy, 'And fetch me a biscuit. Step lively now, or it will be too late.' With a twist of the wheel and a trim of the sail, we barely missed that lee shore. As we rounded the Horn I took the biscuit and bounced it off that cursed rock. Tell that to your grandchildren, lads! Old Toad took you within a biscuit toss of the Horn and pulled you out alive."

The guests were wheeling the Long Tom onto the patio to salute Toad and his heroics as Toad kept it coming...

"I then ordered the crew to set the stunsails; it is off to Siam we go boys; I have a date with the King for tea, and I shan't be late..."

That was too much even for Rat; he had to cut in and get Toad to stand down. When Rat told Toad the bad news, storm clouds as dark as the ones around the Horn furrowed his brow, and he grimly left for Toad Hall.

What conversations took place when Old Toad got home that night... well such matters are best not discussed in polite company.

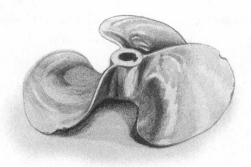

❖ Chapter 5 ❖
Salvaging Toady

"Drudgery is as necessary to call out the treasures of the mind,
as harrowing and planting those of the earth."
ƒ Margaret Fuller, *The Letters of Margaret Fuller: 1842-44*

The next morning Rat and old Mr. Toad glassed the river from The Point, and just as they had feared, the *Runabout* was gone! The rising tide had lifted her from the marsh's gooey grip and set her adrift. They ran over to Mole's cozy burrow and roused him from a deep sleep.

"There is not a moment to lose. Show a leg. Get the gear ready, we must be off. No messing around today. Quick now, step lively."

"I have important business right here," said Mr. Mole as he rolled over and pulled the sheet over his head.

"We cornered the monster! It is running about on the river. Don't you want to corral it?"

"Well...when you put it that way," yawned Mr. Mole. "But I must first have my marmalade and toast....." With much urging and a hasty meal, Mr. Mole was coaxed out the door.

With all haste they threw their ropes and a spare anchor into the bilge and set off upriver. Ratty thought the flood tide would bring the *Runabout* up into the West Branch of The River, so westward they went with the rising sun warming their shoulders. As they rounded The Point and headed upstream, there she was, undamaged, except for a burned out engine, bobbing and twirling happily in the current like a spritely seabird such as a Phalarope.

The benevolent River treated her visitors gently, and, unlike The Ocean on the far side of the dunes, she was forgiving of mistakes. The River had taken this orphaned boat, like so many other boats that slipped their cables, and pulled it softly and noiselessly along on its twice daily rounds, bringing fresh cool seawater up into the furthest reaches of the estuary and exhaling tired brown water into the ocean like the living, breathing creature that Rat surely knew she was.

"I've been tricked; that is no catamount," complained Mr. Mole.

Ratty luffed the sail and brought the nimble *Beetle* athwartship the *Runabout* while Mole secured lines to the brass cleats. Little tendrils of acrid smoke snaked out between cracks in the decking above the engine. A suspicious, but not alarming, amount of water was in the bilge, suggesting some sprung caulking.

Mr. Rat hopped aboard and after much rummaging around and pulling up panels and poking about, he finally found a shiny new, unused anchor. Ratty set the anchor with plenty of scope and then set the backup anchor from the *Beetle* to keep the *Runabout* from swinging onto a sandbar. Then Rat, Mole, and a heartened Mr. Toad (for he had feared the worst) cleaned it up as best they could. Toad elected to stay with the boat while Rat and Mole fetched the launch to tow the *Runabout* into the boatyard for repairs.

That night a grim-faced Harbormaster visited Toad Hall to have a word with poor little Toady. The harangue went on interminably as Toady shrunk into the sofa beneath the towering, red-faced constable. As the Harbormaster explained, Toady had not left a law unbroken: illegal speed on the water, deliberately running over channel markers for fun & entertainment, creating a rooster tail, destroying the marsh, not paying the destroy-the-marsh tax, creating a wake in a no-wake zone, disturbing the peace, operating a boat at night with no running lights, endangering the waterfront, violating the noise ordinances, destroying shellfish beds, polluting The River, and not filing a trip agenda.

Old Toad had been in similar situations himself many times before so he eventually waved the constable off, and the Harbormaster stomped out of Toad Hall with a promise of reform from young Toady. The Harbormaster had his doubts; in years past, promises had been extracted from Old Mr. Toad to little effect; would it be different for this generation?

The next day the *Runabout* was blocked and cradled and winched up the rail tracks as yard workers heaved on the capstan bars and inched her up. The River was happy to be rid of the *Runabout*, and this now notorious boat slid up the rails without a hitch. It came to rest on a set of jackstays, and what a sorry sight it was, waterlogged, bedraggled, and toasted. As Toad and Badger watched, a crane lifted the scorched and seized engine out of the bilge and into a cart. Off the engine went to the scrapyard.

Old Toad's financial accounts had been righted, and he could easily have paid for the repairs, but he had other plans. He remembered that for all the motorcars he smashed up in his youth, he never lifted a finger to repair them. This time it would be different. Young Toady's summer vacation was cut short; no more sleeping in, no more visits to the beach, no more stops on The Hill for ice cream, no more lounging about the estate, no more carousing with Portly, and no more staying up late. And Toady's precious snake collection had to be liberated, and, no, not in little Suzy's yard! Instead young Toady was dragooned into service at the boatyard under his father's stern eyes and Badger's beetling brows.

Every morning, while the catbird excitedly told them about all the berries he was going to steal from their garden, young Toady was rousted out of bed at 4:30 a.m. It was a quick, cold breakfast and off to the boatyard. Mr. Toad always told his son that you must do the worst job first, so young Toady was set to cleaning the bilge and scraping the bottom under the disapproving eye of his father and the glowering Mr. Badger. It was a miserable job, but Toady endured it. Each night he would collapse on his bed at dusk covered in scratchy paint flecks and sawdust.

When he was finished, the bottom was sort of okay. Not too bad, actually. His father's stare was not quite as intense. Badger's scowl softened a bit. When Mr. Toad was satisfied with the scraping, just barely, he had Toady set to work caulking the bottom.

Old Chips, the boatyard's senior carpenter, had taken pity on the young Toad and started to show him the secrets of spinning and applying the oakum to the *Runabout's* sprung planking.

Toady was an industrious, if dissolute fellow, but now he had a clear objective. He began the soothing rocking and tapping of the oakum in the seams. Old Chips took Mr. Toad aside and noted Toady's commendable work. Toad had noticed also, but asked Chips not to congratulate young Toady just yet.

Then came the worst job of all, applying a fresh coast of orange-colored copper bottom paint. It was worse than the scraping, for young Toady was not skilled with the brush and every day his face would be decorated with brownish-orange streaks of paint.

After the painting, Old Toad inspected the work.

"Not bad, not bad at all," he said with the faintest hint of a smile.

So as a reward, it was off to the Hill for Toady's first ice cream cone in weeks and then home.

But Toady's ordeal was far from over. That night the curmudgeonly Harbormaster, who was still simmering, visited Toad Hall with a cartload of damaged channel markers, as well as cans of green and red paint. He had a stern look and a deadline of dawn the next day, so poor, exhausted Toady set to work on the buoys. He got them finished and headed to bed, now speckled with red, green, and orange paint.

The next morning Toady was sent to the machine shop with the dinged up propeller and so began the task of grinding, filing, annealing, and bending the mighty blade, the instrument of terror for denizens of The River. It was sort of interesting work and the torch added a bit of dangerous excitement. Toady actually started to look forward to his boatyard work, and that afternoon he proudly lugged the gleaming prop back to the *Runabout*, staggering under the weight, and bolted it on the propeller shaft.

The next day young Toady set to work on a job that he took a shine to. He worked topside on the damaged brightwork and scratched brass. With much sanding and polishing and varnishing and buffing, the *Runabout* was brought back to its former glory. Young Toady was actually rather proud of his work. His father cracked a satisfied smile when he saw what a job his son had done, secure in the knowledge that Toady's investment in sweat and scrapes and paint stains would pay dividends of responsibility and maturity. For now the *Runabout* had value, hard-earned value, not the hollow value of his father's money, but real value paid for in work. It was something that Toady was rightfully proud of.

The replacement engine, a supercharged twelve-cylinder beast, arrived at the marina in a large wooden crate with the mark of a prancing stallion and stamps from exotic locals in Italy. Along with the engine, a representative from the factory named Enzo arrived to help with the work.

Toady had a far-off, dreamy look as they unpacked the engine. Unlike his schoolbooks, the engine's instruction manual was of great interest to Toady, even

31

if it was written in Italian. The engine was painted bright red, while its muscular, twisted exhaust manifold was dark blue and the valve covers were shiny chrome. This gleaming, beautiful, magnificent monster was hoisted into the *Runabout* as Enzo and the yard workers started fiddling, attaching, adjusting and tightening. Toady helped here also, lending a spanner, clamp, or caliper.

Toady watched in fascination as the engine work progressed; it was the first time in his life that he was ever fully focused on anything. First the engine was attached to an advanced-prototype, turboencabulator drive train. Next all the little attachments, and cables, and pipes and controls were hitched up. After that, there was much tweaking of valves and adjusting of spark gaps and rotating of cams and such.

The time finally arrived for the engine trials. A water hose was screwed to the intake, and the beast was brought to life accompanied by a ferocious throaty, satisfying roar, suggestive of vast untapped reserves of menacing horsepower. The sound echoed down The River banks, shivering windows and rattling teacups. All activity on The River stopped as the youngsters cracked knowing smiles while the mothers and fathers looked up with disapproving scowls. After running the engine for a few minutes, it was shut down, and it was back to more tuning and tweaking and fiddling. Then it was fired up again. This went on all afternoon until Enzo slapped the purring beast, and declared he was finally satisfied that they had it tuned properly.

The crane hoisted the *Runabout* to the skids where she was cradled and wedged. Then she was sent back to a reluctant River. Soon the *Runabout* was proudly bobbing at the slip, the belle of the ball, at least among the powerboats (all the others were slow, conservative, solid-citizen diesel work boats). Of course Badger's Concordia was the undisputed queen of all the boats on The River and would forever remain so, but today the *Runabout* took the spotlight and people from all over town snuck out to take a look.

Soon enough Old Mr. Toad was back to his slow puttering here and there on The River. A week or so later young Toady was seen at his father's side, and it was clear to all that the chastened youngster was back in his father's good graces. Eventually Toady's rating was advanced, and he was handed the helm. On many a day thereafter father and son would set off for a day of fishing and exploring the delightful coves and islands of The River.

The osprey and eiders still eyed Toady suspiciously, but in time they would forgive him. No more roaring sounds at night, no more chewed-up channel markers, no more mini-tsunamis flooding Mrs. Badger's rose garden, no more 10-foot rooster tails of tortured river water shooting into the air, and no more tracks furrowing the emerald brow of the marsh. Peace was restored to the River, or so the residents thought.

Frederick Gorham Thurber

❖ Part 2 ❖
The Delights of Summer

❖ Chapter 6 ❖
The Ratette & The Toad-let

> Love is a madness; if thwarted it develops fast.
> ⨍ Mark Twain, 1898

> "Futile - the winds -
> To a Heart in port -
> Done with the Compass -
> Done with the Chart!"
>
> ⨍ Emily Dickinson,
> "Wild Nights, Wild Nights", 1859

The River history is replete with colorful characters. Toady was certainly one of the most prominent personalities of his era, but there was one other animal that was equally as famous but for an entirely different reason. This was Mr. Rat's daughter, Rickie. No one would have expected that such an unassuming character would play such a prominent role in the history of The River, but she did.

It was widely accepted that Rickie was a bit eccentric, but beloved by the village folk. Much to her dad's dismay, Rickie was not a particularly strong swimmer, but she did love boats and could handle the tiller as well as anyone on The River. She spent many a delightful day cruising The River with her father in his catboat, the *Beetle*.

The clever Rickie loved to solve the puzzles and riddles that her father presented to her. Her grades in school were not so special for she could not stand being confined in a classroom.

Rickie, like her father, was the inquisitive type and liked nothing better than to search for butterflies, wildflowers, and birds along The River. Rickie had a sensitive ear and could actually hear the birds' songs that so many other river residents tuned out. Not only could she hear the birds, but she could identify every squeak, trill, and warble. She even told her dad that she sometimes thought she knew, in a manner of speaking, what the birds were saying. She was relieved when her father took this information in stride; in fact, he confessed to hearing their conversations also and even joining in.

But was there more? Could she hear whispers in the fluttering boughs of the pines, the rustling of beach grass, and the hissing of a retreating wave on the beach? Is that possible she asked her father?

Mr. Rat just smiled at her and said, "Yes, I did hear just such a voice once, The Dream Song, many years ago. I heard it on The River near the Indian shell middens, although I can no longer remember what was said. I do remember it to be haunting and wonderful. I have longed to hear the Dream Song again, but never have."

Although Rickie had developed a close relationship with some of The River's resident birds, she had none with the boys her age, for the birds seemed so much more sensible and polite. These were important attributes that seemed so lacking in the local boys, especially one boy in particular.

Rickie was present during the infamous Mole Crab Incident. The impetuous young Toady had tried the Mole Crab stunt with Rickie, but with surprising results. Toady was rather disappointed when Rickie calmly reached inside her bathing suit, carefully removed the Mole Crab, walked to the water, and gently released it. Rickie then walked up to Toady, gave him the "so-there" look, and said, "Well don't just stand there goggling at me with your mouth agape like a fish. What do you have to say for yourself?" A stunned, bug-eyed Toady could only stare; he was not able to form words. Rickie turned, and with an angry swish of her tail, stomped away. Opened-mouthed, stunned, and silent, Toady was transfixed for minutes. Toady started to regard at Rickie in a new light after that. The more he watched her, the more intrigued he became.

The other boys considered Rickie to be bookish and plain looking. They fancied the glamour gals, the fashion models, and the social butterflies among the local young animals and paid Rickie no heed, but Toady was smitten. In fact as the summer wore on, he grew more and more convinced that he had never seen a creature quite as exquisite as this young Water Rat.

The interest was not reciprocated. Rickie thought Toady was irresponsible, arrogant, reckless, egotistical, noisy, and utterly impossible. She wanted nothing to do with the little amphibian with the big attitude. Rickie brushed him off whenever the love-struck Toady approached her. Crestfallen and rebuffed, Toady would give up for a short while, but his thoughts would always return to the mysterious and unobtainable Rickie.

Toady had a mechanical aptitude and was developing a remarkable skill at problem solving, but here was one tangle he could not unravel. She was about as approachable as the constellation Andromeda and just as cold.

Girls are simply impossible, thought Toady, totally and utterly impossible to understand. Couldn't she see what a perfect match they were? Toady had a great boat with 12 un-muffled Italian cylinders; what more could she want? He could imagine them speeding across The Ocean together with her luxurious, dreamy, chestnut fur streaming out behind her as he revved up the engine with its manly roar echoing off the shore and horrifying the townsfolk — what could be more romantic?

He was good at fishing; he knew all the knots and all the reefs and few on The River could rig an eel skin like him, but it did not seem to impress her. He could catch snakes like nobody's business, but even this esoteric skill did not seem to attract her. His daring exploits were legendary; Rickie should have been smitten, but it just did not happen.

Girls just did not make sense. Girls were inexplicable, impossible, mysterious, maddening, but absolutely intriguing. He figured he had to be bold with his next approach; surely that would impress her. Toady was wealthy and, until recently, pampered, and was used to getting what he wanted, but the one thing he wanted the most was beyond his reach. His father always told him that if you work really hard, you can get anything you put your mind to. But with the dreamy Rickie, it seemed that the harder he tried, the more distant she became. It defied logic. It wasn't fair. It wasn't right. The world was not the logical, well-ordered place that the adults had led him to believe.

❖ Chapter 7 ❖
The King of the Meadow

"I'll tell you how the sun rose,
A ribbon at a time.
The steeples swam in amethyst,
The news like squirrels ran.
The hills untied their bonnets,
The bobolinks begun.
Then I said softly to myself,
That must have been the sun!"

Emily Dickinson,
"I'll tell you how the sun rose", 1865

"A mad, reckless song fantasia,
an outbreak of pent-up irrepressible glee."

Schuyler Mathews,
Field Book of Wild Birds and their Music, 1909

Rickie loved the meadow. If she was ever down in the mouth or tired or discouraged, a visit to the meadow would set her right.

It was not just the wildflowers by day and the fireflies by night, but it was also the theater and the stage for the irrepressible Bobolink. Never had she met one so boastful and excited and cheerful and confident and impulsive and noisy, noisy, noisy. How could you not love a creature such as this?

No bird was so optimistic, so excited, and so enthusiastic as the Bobolink. He simply, absolutely, positively had to tell everyone how delighted he was, from

39

dawn to dusk and from spring to fall. He may look comical trying to balance on a nodding stalk of bluestem, but he would never admit it.

The Bobolinks' words came forth like a sparkling waterfall, one on top the other in a joyous jumble of sounds. His notes went up and down like a county lane on a hummocky farm. He was sunshine and lupines and honeybees and butterflies all wrapped into one.

The Bobolink never skulked around like a timid Warbler, but puffed up his feathers and boldly took center stage. One never heard the sad notes of the Mourning Dove, or scolding protests of the Wren from this character. The Bobolink was never the type to hide like a shy Vespers Sparrow when approached; what did he have to fear? As king, he was proud to parade around in his fancy royal trappings. He lived a charmed life, far from the toil and worry and dirt of the city birds. He enjoyed the best of each season in both hemispheres. When The Hawk came swooping through, and other the birds scattered, the Bobolink could not be bothered; he continued on his cheerful way and wondered what the clamor was all about.

This morning Rickie decided to visit the Bobolink. When she arrived, he ascended to his airy pulpit and preached to the world:

"Is-Am-this-I-not-not-the-the-most-most-beautiful-handsome-day-bird-there-you-ever-ever-was-saw??"

"Calm down, Bobolink. Tell me again. What did you say?"

Bobolink lofted into the air and glided down on shivering wings saying this:

"Am-Is-I-this-not-not-the-the-most-most-handsome-beautiful-bird-day-there-bird- ever-you-was-ever-saw??"

For the Bobolink was so excited to see his old friend that his words ran together, as they are wont to do, one on top of another. The Bobolink was always excited to see anyone, but Rickie was his special friend.

The chestnut-sided warbler may say that he is, "Pleased, pleased, pleased to meet you", but Rickie was never sure if he really meant it. There was no such uncertainty with the Bobolink.

The Bobolink took a precarious perch on a nodding head of Indian grass, looking like a wobbly sailor on Liberty hanging onto a fencepost. He was very sure of himself, but Rickie thought it a bit silly for one so proud to be bobbing up and down on that insubstantial perch. A king needs a throne, not a noodle.

Eventually she got him to calm down and untangle his words; here is what he said:

"I am so happy to see you today, Rickie. Is this not the most beautiful day there ever was?"

Rickie sighed and looked at the proud little creature. Some egotistical creatures were insufferable, one in particular came to mind, but this bird was quite entertaining.

"Every day you say it is the most beautiful day you ever saw."

"Well today is!"

"How about when it is rainy and cold and dreary?"

"That is my favorite type of weather!"

"You said that about sunny days, also."

"That, too."

Bobolink puffed up his feathers and said, "Well isn't every day the best?"

Rickie had to pause. She looked around and saw the ripening bluestem, the lavender bellflowers, the purple blazing stars (her favorite), and the red cardinal flowers. The monarchs were at the milkweed, and the bees were collecting ambrosia at the heliotrope. The oats were heavy with this year's grain, nodding as if to fall asleep in the delicious summer air. Rickie could hear grasshoppers fiddling away and could detect the sun-warmed honey scent of the grass. Maybe the little bird with the big attitude was right after all.

"Hmm, well, maybe, possibly, but it is the same every time I visit. Don't you have a different story?

"Oh the stories I could tell you about my travels, my young friend," said the Bobolink.

"Oh, really, I hope they are not like Mr. Toad's stories. I have already heard too many of them such as: Greeting Amundsen at the South Pole with a warm cup of tea, his discovery of the Mitchell-Hedges Crystal Skull ("The Skull of Doom") in an ancient Mayan ruin, acting as John Wesley Powell's right hand man going down the Grand Canyon, fending off an Abominable Snowman in Tibet with the occult mystic Aleister Crowley on his K2 expedition, being plagued by an ancient Egyptian curse after entering Tutankhamun's tomb with Howard Carter, his friendship with the Lakota Indian leader Chief Sitting Bull, his discovery with Percival Lowell of the canals on Mars, teaching Mark Twain how to pilot a Riverboat on the Mississippi, being serenaded by a Water Ouzel while camping with John Muir in Yosemite, his discovery of the Piltdown Man (the missing link) …"

"No, no," said the laughing Bobolink, interrupting what promised to be a very long list of tall tales, and making note to himself to meet this Toad fellow— his sort of guy. "I wear the proof upon my back."

"Oh, really," said an amused and entertained Rickie, wary of his usual bravado. "Do tell."

"I have flown for days without stopping, to enjoy my repast in the endless rice fields along the coast…"

"Rice fields? I thought you were more of a meat & potatoes type of guy. Do you eat the rice with chopsticks?"

"More like a grasshopper and inchworm type of guy; makes my mouth water to think of it. I don't eat the rice. I eat the yummy bugs that eat the rice. Anyway, may I go on? I was right in the middle of my story."

"Okay, Okay!"

"So, before I was so rudely interrupted, I was saying that from the rice fields it is up again and over the Gulf to Jamaica, whence I enjoy the light music, dark rum, chatting with the Doctor Birds, turquoise coves, tropical fruit, and emerald green pastures. Then it is off again over the Gulf and a long flight across the Amazon basin. After that I follow the spine of the Andes to the fertile Pampas, where I spend the winter with the gauchos, riding horses, enjoying cookouts, telling stories by the fire, and sipping wine."

"Sounds intriguing, but where is the proof, Mr. Know It All?" asked a doubtful Rickie.

"Right here on my back." responded Bobolink.

"How so?" asked a bemused Rickie, steeling herself for one of his tall tales.

"I carry the dark of the Andes on my chest and their snow-capped heights on my back."

"Pffft, that is ridiculous. How can that be proof? You are trying to justify your silly outfit. You look like a butler who put his clothes on backwards." teased a skeptical Rickie.

"So," said the Bobolink, "beautiful day we are having, isn't it?"

"Mr. Bobolink! You are trying to change the subject. I think your coat is ridiculous; you look upside down. Now take the Junco. There is a proper bird; he has slate colored feathers on his back like winter storm clouds and the white on its belly like snow on the ground."

"What's a Junco? What's winter?"

"Oh, brother, it figures you wouldn't know. You are such a fair-weather tourist.

"You are gallivanting around with some gauchos and roasting marshmallows on a fire while we are suffering through the winter. No wonder you are always in a good mood... Now take the Bluebird for instance..."

"Ha, the Blue Jay is a loudmouth, pushy bully. Not a gentleman at all. It is all noise and bluster and carrying on. But what really galls me is that when he decides to nest, it is all hush-hush and quiet and polite, but when others nest he is yak, yak, yak. The stories I could tell you..."

"No, no, I said 'Bluebird' not 'Blue Jay'. They say the Bluebird carries the sky on his back and the earth on his breast."

"That's a lot of responsibility, carrying that sky around all day."

"Oh, you funny bird. You are flipped upside down; a proper bird has light colors on his breast and dark on his back; heck even a trout has a dark back and a white belly. If a trout can figure it out, so can you. The Bluebird has the proper coloration."

"Ah, the true Bluebird. A good neighbor, the finest kind, but very shy, and bookish. Too timid and retiring for me. You would think someone as handsome as that would want to toot his horn. I sure would..."

Rickie rolled eyes, "I am sure you would. And so how do you find your way on all these alleged travels?"

"The stars guide me. One of these nights, and not too long now for I can feel it in my bones, a cool north wind will barrel through our community, rustling the drying leaves in the trees and rattling your windows. Most of you will just put another log on the fire and roll over. Not me. I have to answer the call. On this fair wind, I will set my sail, take a bearing on a star, and be off."

❖ Chapter 8 ❖
Montaup Hill and the Empty Quiver

> "What can poor mortals say about clouds? ..., these fleeting sky mountains are as substantial and significant as the more lasting upheavals of granite beneath them. Both alike are built up and die, and in God's calendar difference of duration is nothing."
>
> ʄ John Muir, My First Summer in the Sierras, 1911

Montaup Hill loomed over The Bay and commanded expansive views of its waters. On its crest was a hardened quartz formation that local children called The Throne. Rickie had a special affinity for Montaup Hill for it was full of birds, butterflies, and wildflowers. When she visited, she was always on the hunt for little treasures such as bird nests, blueberry bushes, lady slippers or arrowheads. Especially arrowheads. There was no better place to find arrowheads than Montaup Hill.

Montaup Hill was an ancient place. It formed in the distant past, before the Age of Mammals and even before the Age of Dinosaurs. Its origins were in a tropical swamp deep in the Paleozoic when amphibians ruled the land and monsters, too terrible to be allowed into the current era, ruled the seas. Over the course of millions of years, miles of sediment buried the swamp.

Compressed and baked and shot through with quartz veins, the swamp was turned into shale and even coal. Montaup Hill's hardened core of agatized quartz was lifted from its foundation by the colliding of continents and exposed to the elements overlooking The Bay. Its flint hard stone stood firm while the surrounding rocks were ground and polished by millions of years of ice and erosion. For eons it had waited and held its own against the gnawing and clawing glaciers. While its brethren were reduced to sand and clay, Montaup stood strong, its crystalline heart of quartz standing up to the strain.

Through the ages, Montaup Hill was a sentinel, waiting, waiting, waiting for someone to hear its story. Humans, with all their conceits, could not hear it; they were too noisy and self-absorbed to listen. Most other creatures could not hear it either for they were too concerned with their day-to-day chores to listen, but occasionally an unusually perceptive animal could pick up a few strains of Montaup's story.

The Wampanoag consider Montaup a sacred place, and it was here that their king, Metacomet, had sat upon its crest and projected his power over the land. The Riverfolk felt an instinctual attraction to this place, and it was a popular picnic destination, especially at The Spring that gurgled forth from the top of the hill.

On this day, Rickie and her father decided to visit Montaup Hill and enjoy a lunch beside The Spring. The waters of The Spring had percolated for thousands of years underground, to only now emerge at Rickie's feet. These waters had fallen as rain millennia ago, when Wooly Mammoths and Saber-Toothed Cats walked the land. Every bubble from The Spring recounted a long-forgotten rain shower, a melting snowflake, water dripping off a Woodland Caribou, or tears falling from the cheeks of the First People. Oh, the mysteries those waters held for ages underground, silent, lost, and hidden, only now to sing their song to the sun and air once again.

As Mr. Rat and his daughter approached Montaup Hill this day, the wind came up from the southwest, and the fog rolled in. The rigging of the trees started to shiver, and their leaves fluttered up, like dancers flouncing their skirts. The ground was damp where the trees had seined the water out of the fog.

As they ascended the hill, they could just barely hear the lilting song of a Thrush. It seemed to fade in and out. But it was neither a Wood Thrush nor even a Hermit Thrush; it seemed to change between the piping of a flute and the singing of a voice.

"What is it Dad?" asked Rickie as she glanced over at him.

But her father was mesmerized, motionless with the hairs standing up on the back of his neck, his nose twitching, and his ears erect.

"Can it be? Is it possible?" whispered Mr. Rat as he stared in awe up the hill.

The piping faded in and out like conversation heard far across a lake. Rickie strained to hear it, and as she listened, words came to her.

"There it is again after so many years," said a glassy-eyed Mr. Rat to his daughter. "We must get closer; I have to find it."

Mr. Rat, at times of exceptional nostalgic clarity, could bring up the seductive notes and words of a dimly remembered dream-song he had heard in his youth on The River near the Indian shell middens. He had longed to hear those notes again, and the prospect of the recovery of a lost treasure from his youth pulsed through his veins as he rushed along the path.

"There! Is that it? It can't be, but it must be. It's the Shepherd, the Helper, the Protector! It is Him, I am sure…" said Mr. Rat in a trance as he looked longingly up the hill.

As Mr. Rat and his daughter listened, they could just barely make out some words:

Listen to me in my faltering hour…

They looked at each other, puzzled and curious. Listen to whom? Why was he faltering?

As they continued up the hill, they caught another line:

My soul was taken on the curlew's wing…

"A curlew? What's a curlew, Dad?" asked the perplexed Rickie.

"A dream, a vision, a hope, a ghost." replied Rat rather cryptically.

"Oh Dad, come on, tell me," exclaimed Rickie, exasperated by another of her father's riddles.

"It is a bird known as the Eskimo Curlew. In the old days, thousands of curlews would seek refuge on the beach during late-summer storms, but they may be extinct now. The last one seen in our area was spotted on a sandbar in The River just before the Great Gale. Your grandfather was a young rat when that storm devastated our community; he set out in his boat to look at the Curlew, but wisely turned back when he saw signs of the approaching storm."

Rat and Rickie hastened up the hill straining their ears trying to catch more of the song, and it came through clearer now:

My soul was taken on the curlew's wing,
Listen to my forlorn heart as it tries to sing.
For like the soaring curlew, we are almost gone,
And upon the barren moor, forever you shall mourn.

Concern and puzzlement wrinkled Mr. Rat's brow, but there was more:

Listen to me in my faltering hour,
My spirit fades, I have lost my power.
Hear my song ere it grows too late,
And eternal darkness pulls me to my fate.

As they approached The Throne, they trembled upon hearing these words:

With an empty quiver I must face the Void
For what has been taken, I will be destroyed.
Within the Hunt our spirits dwell,
You must return them to the shimmering well.

Rat looked at his daughter with concern.

"What does it mean, Dad?" asked the shaken young animal.

"It means that we are on the edge of something momentous, something terrible. We must return home and come back with what he wants. We haven't much time," said a worried Rat.

As they turned and headed for their riverside burrow, these chilling words chased them down the path:

I am the power that keeps the demons from the land,
and stays the vengeful wrath of their scourging hand.
If the flame that once burned so bright is allowed to gutter,
the world you know will begin to close and shutter.

And Orion the hunter in his heavenly attire,
Will drop his sword and to the blackness will expire.

"This is very serious, Rickie, very serious indeed. We must make haste, Little One, before the world as we know it is no more. Our fate and that of everyone else hangs in the balance."

Rat and his daughter quickly repaired to their burrow, gathered what they could find in a rucksack and returned to The Spring.

As they approached, the dirge continued:

I am the guardian at the gate,
If gone, darkness will be your fate.
My spirit will be cast upon the barren field,
And empty souls will be thy bitter yield.
I am in my twilight hour,
fan the embers and restore my power.
Ignore me at your peril,
Beware the darkness it will herald.

Rickie knelt before the spring, reached into the rucksack and began pulling out the flints that she had collected on the hill. One by one she reverently lowered them into The Spring. Arrowheads, spear points, axe heads, hooks, and awls were slowly pulled into the grateful sand, never to be seen again by mortal eyes.

The strident voice they had heard softened and quieted to a gentle whisper. The Guardian and Protector of the small creatures of the Riverfront once again could project his spirit across the land. His quiver had been replenished. As they left for home and walked down the path, they heard one last song:

When the shadbush blooms fall to mold,
Look to the woodcock's fluttering flight,
For there my lonely dance will unfold,
And watch me ascending to the light.

On the way home Rat and Rickie vowed to look for the woodcock's aerial dance when the spring equinox rolled around next year, but for now they had more immediate concerns; they would be on the lookout for Orion in his heavenly attire.

❖ Chapter 9 ❖
Stars with Wings

"Still it wouldn't reward the watcher to stay awake
In hopes of seeing the calm of heaven break
On his particular time and personal sight.
That calm seems certainly safe to last to-night."

ƒ Robert Frost,
On Looking Up By Chance at the Constellations, 1928

"A winged spark doth soar about —
I never met it near
For Lightning it is oft mistook
When nights are hot and sere"

ƒ Emily Dickinson,
A winged spark doth soar about, 1865

That evening Rickie thought it would be good to sit out by the meadow and make sure the stars came out.

"Silly, really, when you think about it, Dad, but why take a chance?" said Rickie.

Rat smiled and agreed. Of course the stars would come out, well, probably. Neither of them wanted to admit that they were a teeny, tiny bit worried after the spooky prophecy they heard on Montaup Hill, so they put up a brave front.

It promised to be a lovely night, and Mr. Rat always enjoyed such outings with his daughter. They set up chairs by the rickety split-rail fence that bordered the meadow and prepared for a languid summer evening. They had mugs of chamomile tea ready, some sweaters against the damp, and candles in hurricane lamps for the walk home. The scene was set. What would happen?

The daylight shift was ending while the night shift was getting ready to take the stage. Rickie and Mr. Rat listened to various birds chirping and chipping their final notes of the day as they jockeyed for positions in their berths. Then all was still as the land paused.

The birds of the meadow went silent, but other creatures took up the chorus. First it was the twangs, like loose banjo strings, of the Green Frogs in the farm pond. Then the little fiddlers started to get ready; this was their time to shine, and they could play their little hearts out without having to worry about becoming Bobolink's after-dinner snack. It sounded like an orchestra tuning up when the Crickets, Katydids, and Grasshoppers started fiddling, but this orchestra would spend the whole night in tune-up mode.

Each creature had a different instrument or tempo, declaring its own space to get their message out, and the evening was soon full of soft trills, clicks, hums and buzzes. The soft, cool airs of a summer night crept in. The earthy scents of the meadow returned after being cooked off by the heat of the day. Dew started to damp their chairs and clothes.

As the reluctant Sun finally took a bow on this fine day, he slipped below the horizon, dragging down his tawny coattails shortly thereafter. The blue of the sky turned gray as the world paused between Acts.

"There it is, there is it, Dad. A star," said an excited Rickie pointing to a bright point in the west just above the departed Sun.

"No," explained her father. "That is Venus, a planet, a wanderer. The stars are fixed in the firmament, but the planets are condemned to ceaseless wanderings across the night sky. And notice, Rickie, how Venus does not twinkle like a star; she has a steady glow."

As they watched, this goddess of the twilight world pushed her shining silver tresses through the lingering gray glow of the Sun and shone brightly over her heavenly domain.

"How about that, Dad, that has to be a star, right?" Rickie pointed to the south at a dancing orange pinprick.

"Yes, indeed, that is a star. It is Antares. Now watch carefully for its brethren in Scorpius, the summer constellation. Scorpius is the constellation of purring Crickets on warm summer nights and the smell of hay on gentle airs. It is the constellation of short-sleeve shirts and straw hats, walking on the beach under the moon, windows left open on balmy nights, friends gathered around a campfire, and boats sliding into their slip after a day on the water. It is my favorite constellation."

And as they watched, Antares's sister stars slowly winked into view. Then the other constellations appeared like ghosts out of the gloaming.

Venus, the overseer of the transition from day to night, watched with her benevolent, steady glow as the cast took their places. As day slipped into night, the players were assembled, the stars were in their proper places, and the stage was set.

Once the nighttime gods, Aquarius the Water Bearer, Cygnus the Swan, Lyra the Harp, Sagittarius the Archer, Scorpius the Scorpion, and the other guardians of the past and protectors of the future had mounted the stage, Venus retired for the night.

With Venus following the Sun below the horizon, the stars could begin their stately pirouette around the Pole Star. There they were frozen in heroic poses, replaying the age when gods walked the earth alongside mortal creatures, or at least that's what The Ancients believed. Within a few months Venus would take up station on the dawn watch and gather her flock, shepherding the great warriors of the sky to their daytime slumbers, but for now she was a goddess of the dusk.

The summer constellations were all in their place, but Orion, the hunter, and his winter brethren had not made their entrance. They were gathering their strength to keep watch over the long cold winter nights to come. Rickie and her father would be sure to greet them when they glided in come November, with the Juncos and winter sparrows trailing behind.

The stars were all out, and Rat had settled in to tell his daughter the mythology of each constellation, but suddenly out of the corner of her eye, Rickie saw a star flicker and vanish.

"Dad! I think I just saw a star blink out!" cried Rickie.
Rat cracked a knowing smile and chuckled.

"Look again, little one. Your stars have wings."

And sure enough, a star lit up, and rose to the heavens. Another dropped to the grass.

It was the Fireflies! They decided they also wanted to celebrate this summer night with an aerial dance. As it got darker, more streaks, blinks, and flashes painted the sky. Other Fireflies joined the melee until it appeared there was a Milky Way of Fireflies above the meadow. It was as if the meadow did not want to give up the stage to the stars in the constellations, and retained little sparks of the Sun's vitality after dark.

Each lightning bug made its rounds carrying a little elfin lantern. Unlike Toady and Portly racing around like dervishes with their sparklers, the Fireflies were cool and quiet. Nature is economical and bent to her purpose; she is unwilling to waste her energies on such extravagances. As Rat explained to his daughter, listen as you might, you will not hear a Firefly—it was like trying to listen to a star.

Rickie marveled at the mass of lights over the meadow.

"What a crazy, mixed up mess," commented Rickie. "Do they ever bump heads or get tangled up?"

"Watch carefully." said her father with a smile.

And sure enough as Rickie watched, she could see that this dance was carefully choreographed. Each little glowing orb seemed to have its own flight lanes and patterns, never getting too close or too far from the others. As Rickie examined these airborne dos-si-dos, she started to wonder if they were all communicating with each other like some alternative community, aloof and alien to all the day-to-day concerns of the river folk.

"It's a dance. The Fireflies are doing a dance!" exclaimed Rickie.

"What kind of dance?" asked her father with a chuckle.

"Hmmm, how about a waltz?" asked Rickie tentatively.

"I am not so sure of that; how can you have a waltz in a hayfield?"

"Why not?"

"High heels & long dresses do not mix well with cow pies."

"Oops," giggled Rickie.

"It must be some other dance," prompted her dad.

"How about a square dance!" said Rickie. She loved square dances.

"Yes, I think you are correct," said Mr. Rat with a smile.

"We cannot have a proper square dance and a hoedown without someone calling the dance steps. And we definitely need a fiddler," said an intrigued Rickie. This is going to be fun she thought.

"Ah, but we have a fiddler, lots of them. Listen carefully."

Rat pointed out that all the clicks, buzzes, and trills from the meadow came from

Grasshoppers, Crickets, and Katydid's playing their own little fiddles. They made their song using their foreleg as a bow and their wing edge as the fiddle.

"Listen," he told Rickie. "There is the Grasshopper playing a soft tune. Hear that delightful musical chirping? That is the Field Cricket. And the buzz? That is the handsome Meadow Katydid. And that lovely, sweet purring is the Snowy Tree Cricket."

"Wow, I had no idea. There is a whole ensemble of musicians right in our yard."

"It's easy to tune them out and most of us do, alas. But oh, what they are missing! You need to listen with new ears and appreciate what we have. Enjoy these melodies now, little one, because one late November night Orion will bring a killing frost and you will wake to the solemn silence of the winter."

"We can't have a square dance without a song and the dance steps. What should we use for the steps?" asked Rickie.

Feigning outrage, Rat asked his daughter, "What? You don't know the "Lightning Jitterbug"? What is today's youth coming to? My goodness, I have not raised my child the right way."

"Dad! Please. I've never heard of it. Nor, I suspect, has anyone else, because I think you just made it up."

Her father just chuckled, "Actually I learned it from your grandmother. It goes like this: First we need to tap our feet to get the beat just right, even if we only have two of them. Ready? Places all; let's go."

> Chicken in the bread pan, scratchin' up dough,
> Grab your partner and start to glow.
>
> Hay's in the hayloft, cider's in the cellar,
> Turn to the left and curtsey to yer feller.
>
> Shine little glowworm, sittin' on a branch,
> Wiggle your tail and make him dance.
>
> Cricket on a fence post scritching out a tune,
> Swing your partner, fly her to the moon.

Froggy on a banjo, picking on the strings
Swing to the sky like a star with wings.

Allemande left, make your lanterns blink,
Turn to your partner, give'em a wink.

Hoot, hoot, hoot, clever ole owl.
Who's awake and who's on the prowl?

Step right up and twinkle your toes.
Round and round 'til the darkness glows.

Look to your friends in the Milky Way
Wing up to the stars and join the play.

"Oh, that is so delightful and so silly! I love it," said Rickie. "Can I add a verse?"

"Sure, each generation seems to add one. I added the 'froggy on a banjo'."

"How about this," said Rickie, for she loved word games, puzzles, and rhyming.

Swing your partner and do those flashes
Paint the sky with your dots and dashes.

"Ah very good, most excellent. Although your grandmother did not know about dots and dashes, I think we should include that in the official version, don't you think? There is no reason we cannot add some modern technology, such as the telegraph, and Morse Code to the song."

"One more?" asked Rickie. "We never mentioned their feet; how about this."

Weave your partner up, and down,
Six little feet, keep 'em off the ground.

"Ha, I like it."

"How about the Whip-poor-will or the nighthawk; we don't want to leave them out. Why are there no stanzas about them?"

"This could go on all night," said her father with a sigh. "I think we have enough verses. The Whip-poor-will stanza will have to wait for another night, or the next generation."

"OK, I suppose we have enough verses. Can we try it out?" asked Rickie.

"Try what?" asked her dad.

"Don't be silly. Dancing to the steps of course."

"It's getting late, but okay."

Rat and Rickie sang the song and did a few dance steps, but their feet tangled and they fell laughing to the ground.

Dancing in the dark would take some practice. It was time to retire.
Rickie had an idea. She told her father to wait a second, lit her lantern, got up and ran back to their burrow. She barely noticed her feet getting soaked by the dew-wet grass. She plunged into their burrow to get her butterfly net and a jar with cheesecloth tied on top.

When her dad saw what she had, he smiled. With a little bit of practice, she found that she could easily capture the little glowing spirits of the night. Soon she was running around the meadow with the net, swish, swish, swish. When the jar was swarming with little lights, they went home for dinner. Rickie delicately put the Leyden jar on the dinner table, and they sat down for their meal. A ghostly glow, the vitality of the forest shining through the glass, bathed Rickie's wondrous face as she peered into the glimmering well of the jar.

"Dad, I want to sleep with the fireflies in my room tonight. Can I, please, please, please?"

"Well, maybe for a little while, but they will miss their friends," responded her father.

After the dining table had been cleaned up and the dishes swabbed, Rickie brushed her teeth and retired to her bedroom with her green goblin light. With new ears, she let the nocturnal fiddlers sing her to sleep.

When Mr. Rat was sure his daughter was asleep, he quietly padded into her room and picked up the swirling jar. He returned to the meadow and released the fireflies so they could join their brethren and continue their dance. Then Rat headed to bed that night secure in the knowledge that all the fireflies and stars were in their proper place.

At about 3:00 a.m. that night, Rickie shook her father awake.

"Dad, Dad, I've got it."

"Got what?" asked her groggy father.

"The whip-poor-will stanza, of course! Do you want to hear it?"

"Ah, hmm, I guess…"

As Mr. Rat drifted in and out of sleep, he heard something about a whip-poor-will that could not stay still, and the listener staying up against his will.

❖ Chapter 10 ❖
The Scavenger Hunt

"We dance round in a ring and suppose,
But the Secret sits in the middle and knows. "
𝓕 Robert Frost, "The Secret Sits", 1942

It was time for the Annual Riverfront Scavenger Hunt, and the community's children had arrived early to gawk at the prizes (the Grand Prize, as usual, was covered by a tarp). Mrs. Badger stepped up to the podium and addressed her charges. In her booming voice, she asked for quiet. The buzz died down and dozens of rapt faces stared up at her in delicious anticipation. Toady and Portly, and his younger brother Stoutly, plus Rickie, Mini Badger, Buck, the Weasel children and all the rest were in attendance.

"Hello to all my lovely little scavengers. Welcome to the Annual Hunt." She looked over the throng and shouted out a question that she already knew the answer to: "Are we ready?"

A roar came up from the crowd.

"Hmmm, are you sure? I can't hear you!"

A louder roar rose from the audience. Mrs. Badger smiled, "That's more like it. So without further ado, let's get started. Do you want to see the Grand Prize?"

A big cheer went up from the crowd. Mrs. Badger pulled the canvas tarp off the prize. Everyone gasped. It was an exquisitely rendered birch bark canoe done in the classic Malecite Indian style. It was small, but just the right size for one of these youngsters. The canoe had ribs and thwarts of steamed oak with a birch bark hull and bent spruce trim. On one side of the bow a Lynx was carefully engraved into the bark while on the other side there was a Rabbit signifying its bravery and confidence in the presence of its enemy.

"Please give a big hand to Beaver and his son Buck, who built this canoe in secret over the winter."

Enthusiastic cheering ensured, for Beaver and, especially his son Buck, were exceptionally skilled wood workers. Rickie was beside herself, hopping up and down and hooting while Toady and Portly stared at it greedily.

"Okay, calm down," said Mrs. Badger with a smile. She then listed the other prizes, pausing after each one for the oohs and aahs to die down.

"Second prize is an overnight cruise on the Concordia to the islands and ice cream cones at Menemsha. Third prize is this brass telescope donated by Mr. Rat. Fourth prize is a treasure chest full of chocolate pieces of eight. Fifth prize is this set of miniature racing cars courtesy of Mr. Toad. Sixth prize is snorkeling lessons and gear. Seventh prize is a pair of tickets to the clambake. Eighth prize is a dozen jars of beach plum jam. Ninth prize is big batch of my special oatmeal cookies..."

And so on down the list of prizes. Since there would probably not be many teams, everyone had a good shot at a prize.

"So, are we ready?" asked Mrs. Badger. "You all know the rules. Ready for our first riddle?"

"Yes, yes, yes," cried the children.

"Okay, put your thinking caps on, my little scholars. Here is the first riddle, and it is worth 5 points. It is a nice easy one to warm up with:

"With this the author can write
And so too the birds take flight."

There was a pause and a murmur, and then a spritely, young Chipmunk named Chirpy jumped up and started running around, dodging back and forth like a bee in a bonnet. "I got it, I got it, I got it.... ...It's a quill! A quill, a quill, a quill, oh wow, I won, I won, I won..."

When Chirpy slowed down, he noticed that his enthusiasm was not shared by the other children. In fact a stony silence ensued as every other child stared at the excited chipmunk with scowls of disapproval.

"Oops. What did I say? Am I wrong? A feather? A feather, right?" squeaked Chirpy.

"No, my dear," said a disapproving, but sympathetic, Mrs. Badger. "The problem is that you are right."

She crossed the riddle off her list with a sigh and said, "Your enthusiasm is commendable my little friend, but let's not spoil the contest for everyone else. I guess I had better go over the rules. Some of you are new to the game and do not know how it is played."

So Mrs. Badger laid out the rules:

• You have to do more than solve the riddle; you have to also find the item that the riddle refers to. First solve the riddle, then find the item, and, finally, bring it to the judges.

• If you know the answer to a riddle, please keep it to yourselves. We know the moment of discovery is very exciting, but don't spoil it for everyone else. If you solve a riddle, gloating and grandstanding, while not strictly forbidden, are discouraged.

• You can work on these riddles yourself or with a team, but no adults are allowed to help. Teammates will share equally in any prizes won.

• You have a month to solve these riddles, after which time please collect the treasures you have found and bring them back here for the final tally.

• Points will be assigned to each riddle. The person or team with the most points will get the grand prize.

• If you happen to find a real treasure chest full of gold doubloons and such, this booty must be shared with the rest of us.

"OK, kiddos, can we try again?"

A roar rose from the crowd.

"Very good. Here we go, for 15 points here is the 'Smack-it' riddle:

"It wears golden bands and rhymes with racket,
which is what you'll make, if you smack it."

There was silence as the little scavengers pondered this latest riddle. Then young Toady, a clever lad belying his family background, jumped up and started hooting.

"I've got it, I've got! I am the Great Toady. Behold my brilliant glow, all of you that are so slow. You best shake off your rust or you will end up eating my dust."

Toady sat down quite proud of himself, but then he saw Rickie scowling at him. Smoke was practically coming out her ears. "OK, Mr. Showboat. We get it; no need to rub it in! It is premature to boast, lest you end up being toast."

Chastised and embarrassed at his outburst, Toady sat down, worried that he had offended Rickie yet again.

Mrs. Badger noted Toady's outburst and said to herself, it figures that he would know that one. "Now children, let's stay calm. There are plenty of riddles to go around. Ready for the next one?"

Silence and rapt attention abounded as the little faces eagerly turned to Mrs. Badger.

"Now for 10 points, try the following puzzle," said Mrs. Badger.

"He has lost his twinkle and cannot shine.
For from the heavens he has fallen
To live forever in the salt and brine.
On five points you can find him crawlin'."

This riddle was greeted by a lot of murmurs and excited whispers.
"That was too easy I see. Well let's move on. For 15 points:"

"A yellow gal named Sue, looks to the sky
And follows the sun with her raccoon eye."

Mystified silence followed this riddle, then some groans and puzzled looks. Less than a minute later Rickie jumped up and started to hop and skip around with her ponytail flying this this way and that.

"So easy. So simple. Ha, ha. I have the lead."

When she calmed down, she saw Toady staring at her. "Well hello Miss Patty-Perfect. Am I supposed to sit and take your rants? It is true that I might be toasted but be careful or you will be roasted."

Rickie turned pink and sat down, averting her eyes. Imagine the gall of that little amphibian, she thought, calling ME a showboat. Offended and embarrassed as she was, she was vaguely aware of some more complicated emotions; she started to think that this little pest was rather clever.

"Well, well, I guess that was too easy. Try this for 30 points," said Mrs. Badger to the oohs and aahs as the contestants started counting the points and realized that this could give them the lead.

> *"Twisting, turning, climbing to the dawn,*
> *Its green fingers lift a velvet bluish horn."*

There was silence followed by groans of despair and complaints about the difficulty. The children looked around to make sure no one had gotten this clue. Once they were satisfied that no one had solved it, they calmed down.

"Not so easy, eh," chuckled Mrs. Badger. "Not to worry; you have plenty of time to figure it out. Let's try another; this one is easy for some, hard for others. For 10 points:

> *"His name is big as you will see, but he is as small as he can be*
> *For in the brine he wants to be, to dart and wiggle in the sea.*
> *On some ice he lays in rows, served with radish from a horse,*
> *Pink and yummy there he goes, get you ready for the first course."*

This was followed my smiles and giggles and whispers.

"Now, now children; no telling. Also remember that we want the specific item described in the riddle, not a general category of things. I think that was too easy. Let's try a challenging one. For 30 points:

> *"With this money there is nothing you can buy,*
> *For it will slip through your fingers if you try."*

The riddle was met with stony silence. The youngsters cast worried looks at their neighbors to see if any had solved this riddle. Nope. No one had, which was re-assuring; this riddle was a tough nut to crack.

"OK, then. I see that set you back; we do not want to make this too easy. Let's try another. For 30 points:

"With bricks and mortar he is bold
But jams and jellies it can hold."

"So how can a 'he' be an 'it'?" squeaked a quizzical chipmunk.

"Mysterious is the grammar; it is enough to make you stammer," answered Mrs. Badger with a chuckle.

"That doesn't help at all!"

"Well my dear, you have lots of time to work it out." said a prim Mrs. Badger.

"Ready for another? For 10 points try this one. Remember we want the specific item, not the general item so listen carefully:

"On his back this plodding fellow carries his house,
You can find him at eye-level for the art-loving mouse."

That caused a mild stir as some children took notes.

"Here is another, easy for some, tough for others. For 10 points:

"Spires of gold reaching upward you might see
But it has no value unless you are a bee."

"We are not finished yet, my little scavies. Here is the last one for 30 points: It is easy if you keep your eyes open:

"Sheds water so you will not sink
But on its pages you can write with ink"

There were a lot of worried looks in the crowd until a Chipmunk exploded in joy and exhilaration; however, she kept her tiny mouth shut, even if her cheeks bulged out as if they were trying to contain the words.

"OK, my little friends, you can pick up a printed version of the riddles here at Scavenger Hunt Central. I will see you in a month. Please register yourself or your team with the committee. Bring your treasures to the judges at any time up to the Counting Day, and we will track them on the Leader Board."

With that the throng paired off into teams and plotted their own little conspiracies. The inexperienced decided to bring in the items that they had decoded right away to see their name in lights atop the leader board, while the other more seasoned contestants, such as Toady and Rickie and various Weasels decided to bluff and feint until the last second, which promised some intrigue on the Counting Day.

Afterwards the parents took their charges home and tried to calm them down, both amused and a tiny bit annoyed by their language change and really bad poetry:

"So you say I should eat my peas, but I'll have just one as a tease and not the whole batch if you please."

"I cannot don my fuzzy jammy, for I find it way too clammy."

"So it's off to bed you say, but I think up is where I'll stay."

❖ Part 3 ❖
The Sea Monster

Chapter 11

The Ocean

"I am tormented with an everlasting itch for things remote.
I love to sail forbidden seas, and land on barbarous coasts."
ƒ Herman Melville, *Moby-Dick or, The Whale*, 1851

"..for ocean is more ancient than the mountains, and
freighted with the memories and the dreams of Time."
ƒ H. P. Lovecraft, *The White Ship*, 1919

While the season progressed with the Scavenger Hunt and other summer adventures, Toady and Portly became increasingly interested in exploring the local waters. After some prompting, Mr. Otter began teaching young Toady and Portly the ways of The River. The boys paid attention this time. When the first glimmerings of responsibility started to manifest itself in the boys, they were given permission to take the *Runabout* on out their own. Toady and Portly spent many lazy afternoons exploring The River, fishing, gunk holing, digging clams, and visiting friends, but The River was schooling them along the way. When Mr. Otter observed their newfound planning and care on the water, he judged it time for the boys to learn about The Ocean. The Ocean is magnificent when in a generous mood, but terrible when it is not. Unlike The River, Neptune is not a forgiving god.

For these lessons, Otter invited them on excursions aboard his solid-citizen, diesel workboat, the *Red Herring*. The first lesson was about the winds. As Otter explained, "the northwest wind brings bright skies and cool temperatures so beloved by the tourist boaters." Otter, the old salt, was not too keen on this wind, for as he explained, this air has to travel hundreds of miles over the land; in the process going in and out of the lungs of numerous other animals first."

"What if those animals had bad breath?" asked Toady.

Poor little Portly turned pink, for he had a bit of a problem with fish breath.

Nope, Otter preferred his air off the sea, clean and fresh. Otter went on to discuss the easterly winds.

"A mixed lot, that," said Otter. "You can feel their brooding, malevolent presence when on the water, but they serve a purpose.

"The Narragansetts considered the northeast wind an evil force, but it is a welcome break during the summer droughts when it brings rain and cool temperatures. In the fall the migrating birds and even fish can ride a nor'easter to their wintering grounds; the waters and shore are strangely silent and melancholy after such a wind has swept all before it to the south. However nor'easters were not to be trifled with, since they could blow almost as hard as a hurricane, and even a moderate nor'easter could be a terror."

As Otter explained, "the southeast wind is an easterly wind but distinct from the northeast wind. It is a wild wind, with none of the tawdry trappings and vapors of the land that the northeast wind picks up. Since it comes directly off the ocean, the southeast wind brings clean air, redolent of the scents and spices of the sea. Even far from the shore, you can enjoy Neptune's cool breath with this wind, but the southeasterly is often a harbinger of rain and wind. The worst storms, even hurricanes, and the heaviest surf come from the southeast as Old Neptune sends his tendrils upon the land in search of his lost children."

Then, finally, Otter discussed the most important and delightful wind of them all, the glorious southwest wind. In the fall it brings welcome respites from the chills. Later it breaks winter's icy grip and brings moisture to parched throats and cheer to wintering animals. In the spring it rouses nature's small creatures and puts air under the wings of the migrating birds to send them north. In the summer it breaks the enervating heat, and stirs the water to bring life to the deep.

"The southwest wind moderates the climate and mood of the land. Have you heard of 'moderation,' Toady?" asked Mr. Rat.

"It is an interesting concept," said Toady. "But it is not something I slavishly adhere to."

"If someone as vengeful and hot-tempered as Neptune can moderate us with the southwest wind, surely a young Toad can also moderate."

When Otter went on to explain the significance of the southwest wind to the Indians, he noticed the boys perk up and pay attention. As Otter explained, the Narragansetts worshipped the southwest wind; they thought that was where the souls of their departed reside.

Otter's next lesson was about the reefs and how to read the water. He took the boys out to visit each reef, giving the ranges, currents and tides for each underwater hazard. First stop was the Sluiceway, a channel between two ledges that sloshed back and forth in a good sea, creating plenty of the white water and current, which game fish seem to love. Next was the Hump, an underwater ridge with various bumps and channels along its flank that seemed to hold fish when the tide was running.

The Washerwoman was next with the whitewater sluicing down her knobby-ridged flanks. Otter explained to the boys that this was old Mr. Toad's favorite reef.

"He enjoys singing a song about it called the 'Ode to Toad' when we fish here. Would you like to hear it?"

"Of course, of course, of course," said a proud Toady, not realizing that his father was a poet in addition to being the world's greatest explorer and adventurer.

"OK, silence between decks there; here it is."

Ode to Toad

Is that a Washer woman or clever Toad, master of disguise?
For he can walk among the unsuspecting, with none of them the wise.

When Toad should appear in his motorized conveyance,
Watch the lords and ladies of the kingdom bowing in obeisance.

The handsome Toad makes the princess blush and bat her eyelashes,
with every derring-do and motorcar he crashes.

"Oh, Mr. Otter sir, my dad never told me about any crashes," interrupted an earnest Toady.

Mr. Otter was silent for a minute or two. The community had done their best to protect the young toad from hearing of his father's wild driving and brushes with the law, but Otter may have gone too far. He tried to recover.

"Ah, yes, good point my young friend. Your father is a great storyteller, the best we have ever had, but sometimes he exaggerates a wee bit. You can rest assured that he was referring to a minor scratch or two in his youth." [1]

"Anyway, there are more stanzas if you are interested."

"Yes, yes," said an eager Toady and Otter.

"You 'axed' for it, so here is the rest:"

Mr. Toad that dashing go-getter,
Across the land, no one is his better.

To future generations, the name of Toad will be sung,
And from the royal parapets his banner will be hung.

For the brave and bold Toad is a hero to the ages,
And in the Great Books, you find him on their pages.

Bold Mr. Toad bears the Righteous Beacon that burns so bright,
It pulls the fishes from the ocean and drives the demons from the night.

Orion in the heavenly realm with your sword held high,
Make room for Toad's star to join you in the sky.

"Wow," said Toady in wonder. "What a great song. I cannot wait to sing it to Rickie."

"Hmmmm," said Mr. Otter, "I am no great navigator when it comes to matters of the heart. Goodness knows, I am more like a poor old hulk on a lee shore when trying to sail those waters, but I think you should, to paraphrase Long John Silver, ease off a point or so on that tack. You would be sailing a bit too close to the wind for that particular wee lass, my young mariner."

"I am afraid I am in stays with her," sighed Toady.

---

1. At this point Otter decided to omit some parts of the ballad such as this:
     Although the judges may shout and scold'm
     There has never been a jail that could hold'm.
There were other verses, some of a sensitive nature, that were so boastful and conceited that, in the interest of good taste, they will not be recounted here.

"Oh, it is not so bad as all that. I think you are trying too hard. Strike the stunsails and double reef that mainsail. What's the rush? Be true to yourself; don't put on airs. You have matured quite a bit since your nocturnal, ah, escapades, and you have earned the respect of your father and others along the waterfront. Eventually she will see the real Toady and stop looking at you as a loose cannon on the deck of a rolling ship."

Toady pondered this a bit, for it was against every fiber of his being to scale back on the pranks and antics.

"OK, Mr. Otter, I will ease the sheet a bit. Goodness knows I have tried everything else."

Toady had one more question, a difficult one at that.

"So Mr. Otter, sir, why is this reef my dad's favorite spot? Why would he disguise himself as a washerwoman?"

Oops, thought Otter, *I should not have mentioned that issue*. Mr. Toad had disguised himself as a washerwoman to escape from jail and commandeer a river barge, but Mr. Toad's checkered past was something the adults were trying to protect the children from, especially now that Toady was starting to develop some of his dad's wild ways.

"Well, Toady, the answer is a bit complicated. When you get older, we can navigate those shoals."

Toady put on his pouty face, for he had heard variations of this line many times before.

Before Toady could ask any more questions, Otter gunned the engine, and they were away.

"OK, boys, now we are going to visit the most dangerous and terrible of all the reefs in our waters. It seems that every fishing region has a 'Widow-maker' reef and ours is called Kerberos, the Guardian of the Underworld."

As Otter explained, it had claimed more victims than all the other places combined. The vindictive Kerberos lurked near the mouth of The River hoping to snare the unwary. It was not just the dangerous currents that swirled around this enormous submerged rock and worked at cross purposes against the daily southwest wind, but it was the shape of this beast that made it so dangerous. It had multiple humps on its back causing confusing patterns of white water. The unwary boaters that ran over to fish the white water on one end of the reef could suddenly find the water under their boat replaced by granite and crunch would go the planking. On the next wave the boat would be lifted up and flipped.

Otter had never actually seen Kerberos exposed at the surface, but only knew of it from the malevolent black shadow it cast underwater and the siren call of the white water it threw out to lure its victims.

Finding Kerberos by looking for the white water was fraught with peril so Otter showed the boys a better way. Otter explained how ranges worked at sea. You lined up some landmark on the near shore with something far away and used that alignment to orient yourself on the water. Just looking at the water, white or otherwise was deceptive, but shore ranges were precise.

For the Kerberos, it was a simple matter of lining up Howland's beachfront cottage with the Inn's flagpole in the far distance; as he explained to the boys, you should never let yourself wander beyond that line, no matter how tempting the water might look. He also noted his arrangement with The Inn: Should they ever move the flagpole, he wanted to know immediately.

The last lesson that Otter taught his young protégés was the ins and outs of knots. Toady learned the clove hitch, the sheep bend, and the square knot. He learned how to do a taunt-line hitch and leave a loop so that it could be released in an emergency with a simple tug. He also learned the fishing knots including the most esoteric of all knots, the mystical Bimini Twist.

But Toady's favorite knot was the bowline, for Otter showed him how to quickly tie this with just a twist of the wrist. Little did Toady know that this knot was to prove crucial later that year. Many, many years later sitting around the fire on a cold November evening and looking at his wife & furry grandchildren, he realized that the few seconds it took for him to tie this knot on that terrible day was the most important knot he was to tie in his life or maybe the second-most important one.

❖ Chapter 12 ❖
The Island

"To those devoid of imagination a blank place on the map is
a useless waste; to others, the most valuable part."
ƒ Aldo Leopold, *A Sand County Almanac*, 1949

It was a calm afternoon and light airs were expected for the next day, so Mr. Toad invited his son on an Ocean excursion the next morning. It would be good to exercise the *Runabout* a bit, he explained, and do a bit of exploring. He wanted to visit some friends, Peleg Slocum and his wife Moriah, who were caretakers on The Island. That night they loaded up bags of fresh corn, wineberries, blueberries (how did these escape the Catbird, wondered Toady), and watermelons as gifts to Moriah, who very much missed such delicacies. Jugs of cider, jars of beach plum jam, and small bottles of elderberry syrup were also packed up along with a newspaper or two, for Peleg and Moriah found the workaday concerns in the news quite amusing.

In the morning before dawn Toad rousted young Toady out of bed. Unlike a school morning, Toady hopped right up, for today promised to be a very special adventure. Before the morning gloaming, even before the birds got up, they loaded the boat, slipped the lines, and headed out onto the glass smooth River. Toad gave his son the helm to pilot them out of The River as he made preparations on the boat. While they plowed the placid River, they watched the sky brighten in the east until the first limb of the orange Sun pushed over the horizon. They left the last of the River's shiny new channel markers behind while the Roman-nosed Eiders on the muscle bar suspiciously eyed the boat. Nervous Cormorants winked and dived, apprehensive when they saw it was Toady's trick at the helm.

Once well clear of the River, Mr. Toad took the wheel and smiled at his son. As he explained, there was a time and place for exercising a boat such as the *Runabout*, and it was not to mow down channel markers at night. Then a gleam came to Old Toad's eye, and he explained that now was the time, and out here they had enough sea room to properly exercise the boat. The fires that had once burned so bright in Toad's heart had not been totally extinguished. It was early, before the southwest wind came up, and they were on the open Ocean before it's brow was wrinkled by a single wavelet.

Mr. Toad winked at his son and asked him if he was ready.

"Give her the spurs, Dad," said an eager Toady.

With a wicked expression and a happy grimace, Old Toad pressed the throttle all the way down. The peaceful chug-chug of the engine changed to a screaming caterwaul as the Roundabout strained at her traces and leapt ahead, throwing Toady hard against his seat. The Eiders scattered as a ten-foot rooster tail of tortured seawater shot up behind the boat. The roar echoed against the shore, while on the beach, Mr. Rat and Rickie paused to cast annoyed looks toward the sea.

Ah, that's more like it, thought Toady. *Oh the joy, oh the bliss, oh the flying miles, oh the freedom, oh the terrified ducks, oh the horrified riverfolk, oh bliss, oh my, oh my; it did not get any better than this.*

The Ocean was slippery smooth with long easy swells. On the crest of each swell, the hurtling *Runabout* would launch itself into air for an exhilarating split second and then come crashing down in an explosion of spray. Most satisfying, thought Toady, as he looked over at his dad who sported a maniacal expression.

The wind in Toady's face made his mouth balloon out and his eyes water.

Midway to the islands, in the deep water near the shipping channel, Toady thought he saw something odd. He tugged at this father's sleeve and pointed. Mr. Toad was intent on making a fast passage and a little bit annoyed to be interrupted, but once he saw Toady's look of wonder, he throttled back. Toady pointed to the east and his father slowly motored over to investigate. Then Mr. Toad saw it too.

Two black shimmering sabers pierced the ocean's smooth surface, slowly waving back and forth like palm fronds.

"What is it Dad? It is spooky."

"It is the Gladiator of the Sea!!" whispered Mr. Toad in a reverent tone putting his finger to his lips.

"Gladiator?" murmured Toady as they got closer.

"A Broadbill, the incomparable Broadbill," said his awed dad.

"A what-Bill?"

"A swordfish," whispered his father.

Toady got very excited and wanted to get the fishing rods out, but his father would not hear of it.

"No, this is too magnificent a fish to hang a hook on; how could you lay out such a creature on the dock, roasting in the sun and being pawed by cats? That is no way to treat such a magnificent animal. As soon as they are caught, they lose their vitality and color. You need to see them in their element. Look carefully because you may never see another one in your life.

"Besides, would you have us cross swords with a gladiator?"

Toady would, but one look at his dad dissuaded him.

As they got closer, Toady could see its cobalt blue body, silver belly and its tremendously long formidable bill. Its huge dark eye, the size of a tennis ball, seemed to look up at them, an eye for the Stygian darkness of a deep realm, not an eye for the air-breathing world of mortal animals. The fish seemed as long as the *Runabout* and had the rakish air of a man-of-war. It was an awe-inspiring sight. "What is a swordfish doing here on the surface?" asked Toady.

"It is on the border of two worlds. Its dorsal fin and tail are in one world while the rest resides in the other. No one is quite sure why they come to the surface, but they do. It is assumed that they spend the night doing battle with the creatures of the deep and come to the surface during the day. They appear to be sleeping when floating like this and pay little mind to boats or baits, at least until they wake up."

The *Runabout* got closer and the fins started to move a little faster.

"Take one last look, Toady, the Gladiator is stirring; the *Runabout* is not exactly a stealthy craft…"

And then with a flick of it powerful scimitar tail, all that was left was an expanding circles of ripples where it had been, like the fading of a dream on waking. So Mr. Toad fired up the engine and pointed the *Runabout* to Woods Hole.

As they flew across the water, the tawny hills of the offshore archipelago gradually hove into view, and Mr. Toad slowed down to navigate the tricky shoal waters of Woods Hole. Toad took this opportunity to point out landmarks and talk about Peleg and Moriah. They tended flocks of sheep on the island and were also "Hen Wardens."

"Why would hens need a warden? Is there a chicken prison out there for criminal birds?" asked Toady. "Some of those roosters are pretty feisty, but this seems a bit extreme."

The word "prison" made Mr. Toad shudder.

"I think I have told you too much already. Let's see if Peleg wants to tell you more about this rather delicate matter," said his father.

Mr. Toad went on to explain to his son that Peleg and Moriah were semi-aquatic boat people like their friend Ratty, but they were a different type of water rat.

In a hushed tone, Mr. Toad looked around, leaned in, and said, "They appear to have a bit of the Pack Rat in them."

Like most of the riverfolk such as Mr. Rat, these were animals of modest means that lived frugally off the land. Out here on this island, provisions and hardware were difficult to find. Peleg and Moriah carefully collected everything they could possibly need and, ahem, some, ah, "stuff" they could never possibly need.

"Better people you will never hope to find", added Mr. Toad. They had been his salvation in his younger days when he and his friend Otter got into trouble on the ocean, which they frequently did.

Occasionally, when there was a favorable breeze, Peleg and Moriah would sail across the Ocean and visit The River community. As Mr. Toad explained, they considered the riverside community a "city", which was rather amusing to Mr. Toad. Peleg and Moriah would shop for various necessities and visit old friends. They were always welcome in town because they had assisted many a mariner from The River when they got into trouble on the Ocean, or just needed a spare part or a fresh meal. Peleg and Moriah made The Island an oasis on a sometimes-hostile sea. However Peleg was never very comfortable with the hustle and bustle of the "city" so after a few hours they said their polite goodbyes and retired to their lonely island.

Mr. Toad and his son took a route through the treacherous Hole where ferocious currents swirled over and around dangerous ledges. Toad motored by an especially nasty looking reef with a pile of black rocks sticking up and the rip tide gurgling and growling over it.

"See that ledge?" asked Mr. Toad.

"Yes, rather scary but fishy looking," responded Toady.

"Correct on both counts! It is called Pine Island," said his father.

"An island? That's a stretch. You cannot call a few slimy rocks an island, Dad!" objected Toady.

"Ah, but it was not always so. My grandfather said that when he was young, this was a proper island, with dirt and land and grass and even, yes, a forest of red cedars. He used to have picnics there; he loved to visit, to fish, look for arrowheads, and those sorts of things. It was a pleasant, green relaxing place with a small beach out of the current for his boat. He said the island was full of shell middens and various artifacts; clearly it had been used for eons by the First Peoples of the land."

"Indians?" asked an excited Toady.

"It would seem that way," said his father then added with a smile. "The Algonquians believe that red cedars hold the souls of their people, and the voices of their ancestors could be heard when the wind moved through their branches."

"What happened to the island?"

"It was taken by the Great Gale. As my grandfather told me, the Gale's storm surge stripped away the trees and soil and undermined the boulders. All that is left are the pitiful remains you see today."

A ghost island, thought Toady. A bit spooky, well, more than a bit spooky, but intriguing.

"It was sort of like Devil's Foot Island there across the Hole; it had trees also before the Great Gale, but at least it still has land."

Sure enough, there was a low scrubby island surrounded by the furious, boiling waters of the Hole.

"The Great Gale swept away all low lying communities along the coast. It came without warning, and its rising waters trapped hundreds. Every house that was not well founded or made of stone was washed away. The ones that survived were wrecked shells."

"By the time the people realized that this was not just another sou'easter, it was too late. There was no time for the shipyards to pull many craft from their moorings. Boats and even ships were pushed onto the land and ended up in pastures and meadows hundreds or thousands of yards from the shore. The wrack line was a mass of splintered wood and flotsam. The Gale created lost houses and lost ships and lost dreams and in some cases, alas, lost lives.

"Many of the underwater reefs that we fish used to be dry land in the past. Fishermen still dredge up mammoth bones and arrowheads on George's Bank, proving that it, too, was once a gigantic island or even a continent. This lost world was taken by some huge cataclysm thousands of years ago; it would have made our Great Gale seem like a sneeze in church.

"So Dad, what is a storm surge?" asked a fascinated Toady.

"It is like a giant, crushing wave sweeping in from the ocean. Hurricanes such as The Great Gale pull the ocean up into their vortex like you pulling your chocolate milk up into a straw. First the shallows are drained of water as the storm approaches and the shoreline recedes. When the storm actually hits, the waters are released and the seas rise ten feet or more. The storm surge causes most of the damage in such a gale.

These sobering thoughts were on Toady's mind as they approached The Island. It was the most beautiful, desolate, haunting place he had ever seen. The Island was dominated by dry meadows, clipped short by the flocks of sheep that Toady could see trotting their way over to see the new visitors. The land was hummocky, full of dips and hills. Kettle ponds dotted the landscape and small pitch pine and beech forests grew in the hollows. The only residence on the island was the caretaker's rickety house. There was also a barn, an icehouse, and a sheep-shearing shed, but no other structures on this whole lonely island.

They rounded a point and carefully wiggled their way into the creek. Mr. Toad killed the engine, and the *Runabout* glided to the dock.

Peleg had seen the *Runabout* coming and was there to catch its lines and tie them off to the dock cleats. Greetings and introductions were exchanged.

Peleg led them up a hill past a bleating flock of sheep, their bells clicking and clacking. Mr. Toad lugged his brass telescope up the hill with Toady in tow. Meadowlarks and grasshopper sparrows flew up as they approached

When they reached the crest of the hill, Toady and his father sat at the picnic table and enjoyed the expansive views of Martha's Vineyard, Nomans

Island, and Cuttyhunk Island. Sailing craft of all descriptions were working the sounds. Toady excitably thought this was the real Spyglass Hill, for here were waters that really had hosted pirates.

The telescope was set up, and they scanned the waters, for this location was one of the best on the coast for ship spotting. Mr. Toad and Peleg had a little story to tell about each vessel, and some may actually have been true. There was a ship from India with spices. Here was another with casks of wine from Madeira. There was a schooner with salt cod back from the Grand Banks. Here was a packet setting out for England. Over there was a pleasure yacht headed to Newport. There was the side-wheeler SS Central America coming back from Panama with a load of gold. Here was a coaster headed to New York. There was a China Clipper, the Cutty Snark, back from Canton with a load of silks and tea. Toady had no idea if this was all true, but it was fun to speculate.

Toady spotted a low-slung, sleek powerboat painted flat black from which they could hear a throaty rumble even up here on their own Spyglass Hill.

"Hey, Dad, what is that dark, sinister boat?"

"That, my son, is our most notorious rum-runner, the *Black Duck*. No revenue cutters have the speed to catch her."

"Could she outrun the *Runabout?*"

"I doubt it; Enzo Ferrari was not the type to ever come in second."

"Look at that poor beat up Barque; is she headed to New Bedford or the wrecker's yard?" asked Toady.

"I'm afraid that at this point, she is more Barque, than bite."

"What's that over there, coming down the Bay, a whaler maybe? Is it off to Tahiti and the South Seas, Dad?" Asked a hopeful Toady.

"It looks like a long-in-the-tooth whaler, but a whaler. Yup, she sure looks like it."

"Can you hear the shanties being sung on that ship?"

Mr. Toad trained the glass on it. "It is named the Wanderer. A bad name to have in these waters; I hope she does not wander off course and onto a reef."

"Hey dad, what is that beautiful ship headed toward The River?"

"That is Mr. Badger's yawl, the Concordia. She is the queen of the fleet, isn't she?"

After a short pause, Toady spotted an unassuming sailing boat headed through Quick's Hole.

"Hey Dad, do you think that oyster sloop is Joshua Slocum's Spray?"

"Unlikely, but possible."

When they got tired of their ship banter, well, actually one never gets tired of such talk, especially from up in the crow's nest of the island, they took down the telescope and headed back. The morning was getting late, and they had appointments to keep. So it was down through the old-growth beech forests on the way back to the Peleg' home. Toady asked his father how the beech trees got there, and he responded that the beechnuts were probably spread by passenger pigeons; by that time the pigeons were extinct, but the trees lived on.

From there, they wandered through incensed airs of a pitch pine grove, past some scotch broom and then through a white picket fence that protected Moriah's garden from the sheep. Next to her garden was their rustic house. The house was clad in cedar shingles tinted gray by the sun and salt. The middle of the ancient roof had a sway back like a broken down mule. Inside, Toady was amazed to see that it was constructed from a hodgepodge of beams and ribs of shipwrecked vessels that had met their end in the treacherous waters surrounding The Island. Few of the beams were of the same size or shape and many still had the adze marks from when they were hewn from field oaks.

Once inside the house, they had a quick lunch, and it was off to see the famous island barn.

Chapter 13

The Island Secret

"The beauty and genius of a work of art may be reconceived, though its first material expression be destroyed; a vanished harmony may yet again inspire the composer; but when the last individual of a race of living beings breathes no more, another heaven and another earth must pass before such a one can be again."

ꬲ William Beebe, *The Bird*, 1906

"The male is at this season attired in his full dress, and enacts his part in a manner not surpassed in pomposity by any other bird."

ꬲ John James Audubon, *The Birds of America*, 1827

"…an island far away to the West and South. It is not down in any map; true places never are."

ꬲ Herman Melville, *Moby-Dick; or, The Whale*, 1851

The barn was a wonder to Toady. He had never seen a building so chock full of odd & ends. Peleg showed the young Toad an old boot that was held together with wooden pegs.

"What do you think Toady? A pirate boot?" said Peleg as he winked to his father.

Toady's eyes lit up, so Peleg discussed the local pirate legends.

"These lonely, deserted islands were naturally quite alluring to pirates, privateers, renegades, fugitives, weasels, and other outlaws. Piratical types had been seen all along the shore for centuries, sometimes anchored up, and sometimes even going ashore (for fresh water or was it to bury chests of gold?). Tarpaulin Cove was a favorite landing place for pirates and British men-of-war, but no treasure had ever been found at Tarpaulin or elsewhere along the other islands. There were hints and rumors and clues, but nothing concrete had been discovered, at least not anything that anyone wanted to talk about."

"So Peleg, don't you have a real treasure here on the Island that you can show Toady?" asked Mr. Toad.

This question was met with silence as Peleg took on a stern expression, looking back and forth between Toady and his father.

"Mr. Toad, is your son ready? Can he be trusted?" asked Peleg.

"Yes, he has been through some tribulations, but has proved himself in the end," said a proud Mr. Toad.

"OK, Toady," said Peleg. "But remember that what I am going to show you is the most important secret you will ever learn, even more important than those secret fishing holes back home that Otter showed you. It is a secret that has been closely guarded for generation after generation here on the islands. If the secret gets out, the treasure will be destroyed and lost forever. Do you understand?"

Toady solemnly nodded his assent.

"OK, this way then."

Peleg led them deep into the interior of the island about a half-mile from the shore, far from any prying ship-bound eyes. As they walked Toady could hear strange, haunting, spooky piping sounds like a foghorn or the sound made by blowing over the top of a bottle. There seemed to be hundreds of these strange toots coming from the center of the island. Toady asked what it is was.

"It is the booming; you can hear it for miles."

Something peculiar was going on, thought a mystified Toady, *very, very peculiar*. As they got closer to the middle of the island, they started to hear clucks, cackling, chuckling notes, and kazoo-like sounds. Closer still Toady started to hear drum rolls. There was something really odd about this island, thought an intrigued Toady. Was there a miniature army of redcoats mustering on the island before invading the mainland?

As they entered a flat plain of sandy grasslands interspersed with stunted oaks, Peleg said, "Here it is, the Lek."

Toady was expecting a treasure chest or a gold mine, and was unprepared for what he saw. Cavorting on the ground were the most peculiar and comical and altogether delightful birds he had ever seen. These grouse-like birds were about the size of a Rhode Island Red rooster, but oh so much more beautiful and exotic. They were prancing, pirouetting, strutting, stomping their feet, dancing, puffing up, challenging their brethren, tooting, and basically showing off for the ladies. The males appeared to produce the booming from puffed up red sacks on each side of their necks.

What really struck Toady about these birds was their "ears" which were actually feather tufts on each side of their necks. They looked like rabbit ears but were much more expressive. They flashed up into an inverted V, down, forward, and, most comically, straight apart to stick out the side of their heads. They could strike so many poses that he thought he could watch them for hours.

As Toady carefully observed their antics, he was reminded of a Sioux Indian war dance. The male would lean forward, all tense and stiff with its tail feathers held high like a flashing deer. Then this amazing bird would rapidly stomp its feet and slowly wheel around all puffed up and tense. The pattering of his feet sounded like the rapid beating of a drum.

"What are those crazy birds?" asked Toady with a laugh.

"They are Heath Hens, and they are 'lekking'. A lek forms when the males congregate and try to out-do each other in the hopes of catching the fancy of one of the ladies. It is one of the greatest shows that nature has ever staged.

"What you are watching is one of the most endangered birds in the world. The Passenger Pigeon, Carolina parakeet, Labrador Duck and Great Auk are now extinct while many others such the Eskimo Curlew, the Snowy Egret, and most ducks are almost gone. This is the only safe refuge left for Heath Hens. Martha's Vineyard has the only other colony of Heath Hens, but those birds are almost gone, wiped out by fire, storm, and Goshawks.

"Here in front of you is the last stand for these birds. No one knows about the existence of these Hens, not the bird watchers, not the state biologists, not the fledgling Audubon society, certainly not the hunters, and not the ornithologists at the universities, who are almost as bad as the hunters. This meadow is a blank spot on the map, and we intend to keep it that way. As long as you keep the Hens' secret, they will be safe from the meddlers, the collectors, the birders, the jabronis, the curious, the 'sportsmen,' and the poachers. It is our deepest secret here on the islands and our greatest treasure.

"Heath Hens used to be common all through our area. Many, many years ago they were to be seen scampering around the Boston Common! They were so abundant that colonial servants and laborers had an agreement with their masters that this bird could be brought to the table no 'oftener than a few times a week.' The Heath Hen has been gone from the mainland for a century at least."

"What about laws and regulations to protect the Heath Hen?" asked Toady. "Surely they could have been protected?"

"Laws were enacted, but they were too little and too lax and too late. Some of the laws were even repealed, but most were just ignored, such was the vision of men who could see no further than through the sights of their guns. It is the same myopia as the fishing regulations today; the laws do nothing except give the illusion of protection while allowing the greedy to continue their depredations."

As Toady considered these sobering thoughts, he kept watching the Heath Hens. He noticed that there were female birds mixed in the flock, but they were busy picking up grasshoppers and were not the least bit impressed by the antics of the males. That must be frustrating to the males; all that trouble for nothing. *Hmmm*, thought Toady, *sort of like me and Rickie; maybe Mr. Otter is right, and maybe I need to ease off a point or so.*

Toady did have one more comment.

"I know a certain young water rat who would really, really love to see these birds." suggested a hopeful Toady.

"No, not yet. Someday, maybe," said Mr. Toad.

Peleg went on: "Humans cannot be trusted with such knowledge, for their greed and competitiveness will have the better of them. Even well intentioned people will still try to poke and prod and band and meddle; we saw how that worked on Martha's Vineyard. No, this is a secret for Water Rats, Toads, and the like. Animals can keep a secret, and we have many that humans will never know. In time I am sure we can show your young friend. Animals need their secrets and private places. Humans do not know it, but they also need blank places on the map and unsolved questions, but watch how quickly they would sell out this spot and these birds if they knew."

The day was getting late, so the Toads said their goodbyes and were off.

Little cat's paws of an awakening southwest wind were making their way up the Sound, so there was not a moment to lose. They fired up the engine of the *Runabout*, cast off, and motored down the channel to the Ocean and straight home. The southwest wind started to build, as it is wont to do on such a splendid bluebird day and flecks of white started to cap the indigo waves. Overhead, Mackerel skies and Mare's tails watched their return, sending down shifting shafts of sunlight on this waning day. By the time they got to the River, a double-reefed topsail breeze was blowing. Mr. Toad and his son surfed down the face of the waves, burying the bow in the next wave then pulling up, and repeating it again and again. So they came into the River on a bucking stallion with a roaring engine. Then the beastly engine was throttled back to a slow thob and peace returned. The kindly River took the two Toads back into its warm embrace.

That night an exhausted Toady flopped on his bed and was instantly asleep. He had vivid dreams of a gladiator crossing swords with his father, pirate boots dancing a jig, and an ominous ghost island rising out of the sea. Who would have imagined that the last dream would actually come true?

❖ Chapter 14 ❖

Perseus' Spear

"The beauty of a butterfly's wing, the beauty of all things, is not a slave to purpose, a drudge sold to futurity. It is an excrescence, superabundance, random ebullience, and sheer delightful waste to be enjoyed in its own high right."
 ℰ Donald Culross Peattie, *An Almanac for Moderns*, 1935

The Perseids Meteor Party was one of the highlights of summer, and this year promised to be special since the moon did not come up until late that night. Mr. Rat had worked out the date for the meteor shower, and all the animals marked their calendars. This party was an excuse to enjoy the relaxed pace of a night on the beach after all the hustle and bustle of the working day. Here the Riverfolk could kick back, enjoy a cookout over a driftwood bonfire, and watch the show. The children especially loved this party since it gave them an excuse to stay up late and enjoy the spooky wonders of a nocturnal beach.

The personality of the shore changes at night. During the day it is a tumult of frantic activity; it is all Gulls and Terns and crashing surf and youngsters screaming in delight. Everything is bright and vibrant and full of energy when the sun shines. At night the mood on the beach changes. Instead of a shore bustling with birds and bathers, there is the solemn stillness of gentle surf quietly being watched by the stars overhead.

That day a palpable excitement was in the air as friends met on the shore at dusk. The southwest wind had faded to a whisper, and the ocean had flattened out. The air was thick with the scent of heather, pitch pine, sweet fern, rose hips, and Neptune's breath from the sea. It was a languid night, and even the waves seemed sleepy and slow; they sounded like gentle, polite clapping between arias of an endless, rhythmic opera.

There was a twinkle to Mrs. Badger's eye during the preparation and even the hint of a smile for she loved children, even the high-spirited ones (up to a point), and this was the happiest night of the summer for the youngsters. She remembered when she was a young Badgerette, and she got to relive the magic of a picnic on the beach at night. Mr. Badger could be gruff and a bit of a curmudgeon with adults, but he enjoyed the antics of the children, even Toady and Portly, except for the Mole Crab Incident, of course.

Rickie walked over to check on the mermaid that she had created a few days before. She was miffed to find that someone had put a cigar in the sweet mermaid's mouth and added bushy black eyebrows and a moustache; Rickie was pretty sure she knew who the culprits were, based on the cackling and snickering she heard from the Weasel children. Toady saw this too; he ran over, pulled the cigar from the mermaid's mouth and threw it in the sea. Then he exchanged some sharp words with the disrespectful Weasels and had to be held back by Portly lest the hostilities escalate.

As Toady turned to head back to the party, he saw Rickie staring at him. It was not the usual scowl, and it was not quite a smile, just a stunned, puzzled sort of look. Toady floated on air the rest of the night. In the following days, Rickie did not pop his bubble, but without further encouragement, it gradually deflated.

An elaborate fire pit was built for roasting the food. A circle of rocks was made in the sand and a hole was excavated for the campfire. The pit was lined with cobbles to hold the glowing coals. The youngsters were sent into the dunes to gather dried boughs of pitch pine while the older animals fanned out along the wrack line to collect heavy hunks of driftwood. This was the Age of Sail and driftwood was abundant. Here along the shore they found the bones of long forgotten ships (and dreams): white pine spars, pasture oak knees, chestnut ribs, yellow pine beams, lignum vitae blocks, and cedar planking, set adrift so many years ago, now returned to their natal shore.

The driftwood had come from trees pulled, against their will, from forests, fields, and swamps, like reluctant farm boys rounded up by press gangs to serve in the Navy, but, oh, the adventures these trees had experienced! While their neighbors had fallen and moldered on the floor of some wet wood, these trees had set sail across the globe. They had traveled the seven seas and strained against innumerable gales, felt the bare feet of sailors called to quarters, been scoured by holystones, been rent by cannon balls, and listened to sea shanties as the crew strained at the capstan bars.

Now, after their wanderings, they had returned for one last glorious celebration, to light up the faces of wondrous children around a campfire. Sunlight so patiently captured and stored in their sinews for decades was released; this investment of the sun's nurturing rays played its final act as its light was released at last to celebrate the fireworks to come overhead.

The fuel for the fire was carefully constructed into a layered mound while the youngsters eagerly watched. Crisp dry straw was laid down first. Then bundles of cedar kindling were unpacked and laid on the straw. Next came a huge pile of driftwood stacked in a teepee shape over the pit. Finally, some pine logs were laid on top to add their essence to the meal. A stack of pitch pine was laid aside as a reserve when the fire got low.

While the children were busy with laying down the fire, Mrs. Badger, that benevolent tyrant, assumed her customary role as the Field General in charge of the cooking. She directed the campaign with her commanding voice, cutting through the noise and marshalling the troops. The village folk teamed up to carry the heavy picnic baskets along the path, and the provisions were plopped down next to Mrs. Badger's command tent. Then the serving tables were assembled. The tablecloths were laid on the tables, and the beach plum and elderberry jams, apple butter, and beach rose treats were put out. The fire was started and soon enough the first tendrils of resinous smoke drifted up from the piled wood. Viewing spots for the shooting stars were chosen in the sand, and blankets were rolled out.

The first baskets to be opened held the watermelon. A bit of the winter's coolness was carried to the beach that night, for the baskets were packed in ice harvested from the Ice Pond in January. Mrs. Badger opened the heavy baskets, pulled back the straw insulation and reached in for the cool slices as the children eagerly waited in line.

Then it was a melee as the happy children ran off with their treats. Rickie was disgusted when she saw Toady and Portly, engaged in a contest to see who could spit the seeds the furthest with lots of sound effect, histrionics, and laughing.

"Must they do that, Dad?" She asked.

"I am afraid so," chuckled her father.

"You never did that when you were a boy, did you Dad?"

Her father just smiled.

While this was going on, Otter, Rat, Mrs. Badger, and the other strong-handed Riverfolk got to work shucking oysters and laying the half shells on a tub of crushed ice.

As the sun said its last goodbyes to this fine day, hurricane lamps were lit and hung from branches pushed into the sand.

Now it was time for the meal. First came the oysters. They were plucked from their half-shells, wrapped in bacon, and put on long skewers to be laid over the fire. Soon enough they were dripping and sizzling, tempting the guests with their succulent scent.

Next came the freshly picked corn still in its husks (generously donated by Mr. Woodchuck). It was delicately placed on the coals with long tongs. In this way the steaming corn became imbued with the charcoal of the driftwood and resinous scents of the pitch pine. Within minutes everything was ready.

A line formed as the Riverfolk queued up with their plates, and Mrs. Badger got to work giving each animal a skewer of oysters with an ear or two of corn. Salad was added for those who wanted it, which did not include Toady and Portly, of course; they were all about the corn. The adults were given mugs of either punch or rose-hip tea while the youngsters got paper cups of lemonade. Bread was toasted over the fire on toasting tongs and spread with Mrs. Badger's special beach plum jam (sweetened with Madeira). Then the throng retired to their beach blankets to enjoy their meal and settle in for the show as the moths flitted around the hurricane lamps and cast a flickering light on the crowd.

When dinner was finished, the plates were collected and the adults lay back on their beach blankets with relaxed sighs, but the children were excited by the prospect of dessert. Special treats, tucked away and carefully guarded by the redoubtable Mrs. Badger, lest some of the youngsters jump the gun, were brought forth. The basket of marshmallows, chocolate, and graham crackers was opened and laid out on the serving table. Fresh cut yellow birch sticks, redolent of wintergreen, were distributed. Spearing a marshmallow or two, the youngsters crowded around the fire.

As Mr. Rat looked at the glowing faces of the expectant children, a deep contentment came over him. This, he reflected, was what made those long winters, hauling and splitting firewood, sledging ice from the pond, and shivering around the hearth worth it.

Rickie put a marshmallow on her stick and gently rotated it above the fire; it was a matter of pride for her to not let it catch fire, and she delicately toasted it to a golden brown. The boys had a different idea; Toady and Portly ran around the beach with flaming marshmallows held aloft like torches, finally downing the carbonized treats when they went out, leaving sticky, blackened streaks on their lips and chins (As the boys realized the next day, they had also singed the tops of their mouths, but they hardly noticed it at the time, such was the excitement). Then it was back to Mrs. Badger for more marshmallows. And so it went until the supply ran out.

The hurricane lamps were turned down a bit and a reverent hush fell over the party. A light clearing northwest breeze had come up which seemed to fan the stars like embers and make them sparkle with crystalline intensity. The twisting streams of smoke from the fire lazily headed out to sea. Even the chattering and chortling of Toady and Portly slowed down. The only sounds were the rhythmic pulsing of the light surf, the chatter of the little Sanderlings chasing each wave, the occasional pops of Striped Bass in the ocean, and the crackling of pitch pine on the fire releasing the sound of some long-forgotten thunderstorm

The Milky Way blazed in the sky, stretching from the northern horizon all the way overhead and finally plunging into the sea to have it's fires quenched.

Most of the crowd lay back on their beach blankets to wait for the show to start. Every ten minutes or so, Toady and Portly would add some pitch pine boughs to the fire; the fresh firewood hissed and popped, sending sparks high into the sky. In minutes the spendthrift boys released the warmth and light that the pines had collected so patiently from the sun.

And then it happened: Perseus began throwing down his bolts upon his unseen foes. First with a silent thread of light, so subtle that those who saw it did not quite believe it. Then another and another. Each flash drew gasps and comments such as: "Did you see that?" "Where?" "There." "Too late!" "Oh, another!"

Occasionally a meteor would leave a bright lingering train of glowing debris. The biggest gasps came from a shooting star that was so bright it lit up the ocean and beach for a brief second before its fires were seemingly extinguished in the sea.

Rickie was lying back on her beach blanket looking at the sparks from the campfire traveling up and meteors traveling down.

"So Dad, what's the purpose of these shooting stars?"

"See the constellation to the right of Perseus? That is the beautiful Andromeda, and Perseus was madly in love with her, you know. Perseus is protecting her from Cetus, the sea monster. The meteors are thrusts from his spear."

"Daaaaaaaddddddd, did you make that up?" asked Rickie.

"That is what the Ancients believed; I only embellished it a bit. It seems like as good explanation as any," responded her father with a chuckle.

"Dad, I don't really believe that Perseus is up there swinging his spear around, nor do I believe in sea monsters."

"I believe in sea monsters," said Mr. Rat. "I don't know if you realized this, but we have our own sea monster right out there beyond the surf line; it is a reef called Kerberos. Who is going to protect you from that sea monster?"

"Dad! Please, I can fend off any imaginary sea monsters, and I don't need a Perseus, thank you very much," said Rickie (as it would turn out, she was wrong).

After a pause, Rickie added, "Dad, I need a more realistic explanation of the meteors."

"Maybe it is sparks flying from Vulcan's forge," suggested Rickie's father.

"What is he forging?"

"Orion's Sword"

As of late, Orion had become of great interest to Rickie.

"Hmmm, interesting, but I am not so sure," said Rickie.

"Or maybe the stars get tired up there or bored just hanging around and let go like apples in a storm."

"Now seriously, Dad, that is ridiculous."

"At night on the beach, your pupils open up, but you also need to let your mind open up."

"I am still unsure about those meteors."

"Just don't hitch your wagon to one of those falling stars," added Mr. Rat with a chuckle.

"Oh brother, I wonder who you could be talking about," said Rickie with a sigh.

Rickie lay back and watched the sparks from the campfire head to the heavens.

"So Dad, do the sparks from the fire on the way up, pass the shooting stars on the way down?"

"Interesting, I had not considered that," said Mr. Rat.

"What do they say in passing?"

"Oh I don't know, maybe a tip of the hat, a good-day, and they go about their business."

"Wouldn't it be simpler if they just stayed put? Why can't they be content where they are?"

"I have asked that very same question myself to various local animals, but rarely had a satisfactory answer, or at least one that I could agree with. I never thought to ask that of a spark or a shooting star. The next time I meet one on the road, I will ask."

"Daaaaadddddd…"

"I am content where I am along the River, but others feel a call that I will never understand. Some animals are never satisfied with their place and hobo around looking for better lodgings but never finding them. Others, like the shorebirds feel the pull of the departing summer constellations, and some, like the Warblers get restless with the shorter days. Some fish, such as the Striped Bass, don't like the cooler water and autumn storms. Many birds including the Barn Swallows need tasty bugs to dine on and travel to warmer climes in the winter to search for them. Others, well I just don't understand."

Rickie saw a bird fluttering at the hurricane lamp; she tugged at her father's sleeve and pointed to it. On closer inspection, they found out it was not a bird at all, but a huge moth the size of a salad plate. Rickie had never seen anything so hauntingly beautiful.

"What is it Dad? It is lovely."

"That is a Luna Moth, one of the Saturn moths. I was hoping we would find one; they are rather rare these days."

The Luna Moth had four green eyespots, with what looked like red and black mascara, on its delicate wings. The eyes on the hind wings sort of winked with every flutter. It had two long tails like a Barn Swallow but twisted a bit. On its head were two curved feathery antennae (to sniff for a lady Luna Moth's perfume explained her father) attached to a white furry head and body. Its pinkish legs wrapped around Rickie's finger when she reached for it, and perched there slowly flapping its wings like decorated oriental fans. What really struck Rickie was the color; it was a ghostly elfin green, like her firefly jar back home.

"So Dad, why is it so beautiful?"

"Probably to attract a lady Luna Moth."

"Isn't it interesting that what passes for beautiful in the insect world is also beautiful in our eyes?"

Rickie saw that far-off look in her father's eyes, and braced herself.

"Rickie, my dear, that is the most profound question you have ever asked me. It speaks to the universal nature of beauty, or is it the universal beauty of nature, hmm... oh bother, where was I, ah, yes, it speaks to the universal nature of beauty that transcends species boundaries..."

Oh-oh, thought Rickie, now I have done it; Dad is off on one of his tangents.

"...And even may transcend life itself. Consider for a moment the evolutionary gulf, the vast abyss if you will, between that seemingly primitive moth and the supposedly higher animals that we imagine ourselves to be. Somewhere back in the infinite recesses of boundless time..."

Oh no, Dad is really getting geared up, thought Rickie.

"Somewhere back in the infinite recesses of boundless time, maybe even in the primordial ooze, there was a common ancestor, long gone and forgotten, of both Moths and Water Rats, yet when they diverged, could each of its descendants have carried the same aesthetics of beauty? Or is beauty more universal than that..."

At this point Rickie lost the thread, only catching bits and pieces of her father's talk. With glazed over eyes, she watched the fire as it hissed and popped sending sparks into the air.

" ...Consider for a moment the image the lady Luna Moth sees of her mate... As you can see Rickie... Rickie? Rickie?"

Rat looked over and noticed that his daughter was asleep. Mr. Rat sighed and leaned back in his chair. Preaching to the stars again, he thought.

On this night the meteor show was not to last. Soon the nosy Moon climbed out of the Ocean to see what all the excitement was about, but only washed out the show. It was time to go and tuck the youngsters into bed. Lanterns were turned up and their glowing wicks cast a dancing light as the parents walked single file down the soft path, some carrying sleeping children wrapped up in blankets. They wended their way through the deliciously spooky and mysterious dunes under the dark boughs of pitch pines with the Moon sending silver shafts of light down on them.

Before they left, Mr. Rat looked up one last time and tried to count the stars to make sure none were missing. They all appeared to be in place, or at least it seemed that way.

◆ Chapter 15 ◆
Plum-backed Swallows & Winded Warblers

"The swift-winged swallow sweeping to and fro,
As swift as an arrow from Tartarian's bow."
ƒ William Wood, *New England's Prospect*, 1634

"All Nature is linked together by invisible bonds and every organic
creature, however low, however feeble, however dependent, is necessary to the well-being of some other among the myriad forms of life."
ƒ George Perkins Marsh, *Man and Nature*, 1864

The night had been crisp and clear as Rickie went to bed. The next morning,
just as the sky was beginning to lighten, a Carolina Wren took up station outside
her window and started yodeling. From her bird books, Rickie knew that the
Wren was supposed to be saying, "Teacher, Teacher, Teacher"

However, Rickie thought that this bold Wren, a half-ounce drill instructor,
was instead saying, "Get Up, Get Up, Get up!"

Rickie could not believe that so much noise could come from such a tiny
pinch of fluff. She got up, "shushed" the Wren, closed the window, and headed
back to bed. The cheeky Wren responded with some outraged scolds, and went to
another open window.

"Time To Go, Time To Go, Time to Go."

Rickie rolled over and pulled the sheet over her head.

"Lazy-bones, Lazy-bones, Lazy-bones."

"Ugh. Why can't you sing in the spring like a proper bird?" asked Rickie. "It is too late in the year for this foolishness. Even the catbird has slowed down to a few meows in the morning."

"Out Of Bed, Out of Bed, Out of Bed," yodeled the impertinent Wren.

"What's so great about today?" asked Rickie

"Gonna-miss-it, gonna-miss-it, gonna-miss-it"

It was no use. He would not let her be.

She collapsed on the bed and stared up at the pine paneling on the ceiling of her bedroom in frustration, imagining what the swirls and knots of the wood represented. There was a cyclone. Here was the beak of a hen. There was the curl of a breaking wave. Here was a knot that looked like a rock in a stream. There were two knots like eyes looking down at her, glaring at her. They were the eyes of a....no...No...NO...NO...the beady eyes of a Toad, staring down at her! She shot bolt upright. Any more sleep this morning was hopeless; this day would not be denied its audience.

So Rickie reluctantly slid out of bed and headed to the kitchen. When the Wren saw this, he retired to the shed to take a nap, his mission accomplished, or at least that is what Rickie ruefully thought. *Maybe I will visit him tonight in the shed when he is sleeping,* thought Rickie, *and practice my violin for the impetuous little twerp.*

It was the high season, and the table was well stocked with produce from the garden. Rickie enjoyed a breakfast of peaches, fresh hickory nuts from their tree in the yard (named Old Shaggy), blueberries that were netted against the Catbird, blackberries, and fritters made from fresh corn.

Rickie's father joined her at the table, all bright-eyed and bushy-tailed, but the groggy Rickie had to ask the obvious question.

"So Dad, why does the Wren have to wake up as soon as the Sun rises? Why can't he sleep in?"

"Funny that you should look at it that way. I always thought it was the other way around; the Sun, like you, does not get up until it is called out of bed by the Wren."

"Oh Dad, don't be ridiculous. What happens in the winter when the Wren has stopped singing?"

"Ever notice how late the sun comes up in the winter? Like a teenager, the sun simply cannot get out of bed without the Wren to wake it. Then, in the spring, when the Wren starts up, the sun simply leaps out of bed, full of excitement and promise. As a scientist it is pretty clear that it is the Wren who wakes the Sun, not the other way around."

"Oh bother, I can see you are in one of your moods. Will I get a straight answer out of you today?"

"I could answer that, but it would not be straight."

Although Rickie had objected to the Wren, the pipsqueak troubadour was right; this was a special day. The season was changing and the world was on the move; Mr. Rat and his daughter had an expedition to go on.

The woods were hushed now and every sound seemed to echo dully like a hymnal dropped in an empty church. There were no warblers or thrush singing at the spring on Montaup Hill. There were no swallows over the Ice Pond. The bluebird boxes were empty and the yellow warbler nests were vacant. The frantic rush of the new season was over, and birds that were still left were quietly concentrating on fueling up for the long journeys to come. The only consistent sound was the bubbling of The Brook, and the rustling of the cedars in the breeze. An occasional flock of kinglets moved through looking for insect eggs, but it was all chips and whispers and clicks and secrets. Starting in the late afternoon and going until early evening, the Great Horned Owls, those fearsome rulers of the night, began marking their territory and asking who was awake. Little else disturbed the solemn, dignified stillness of a forest in repose.

Splashes of color were beginning to checkerboard the green cloak of the leaves, like miniature sunsets drawing the curtain on the season. The trees were about to begin their long slumber, to be awakened in April by the warm caress of a southwest breeze and Pine Warblers whispering in their ears. What those warblers said to the trees to stir such a mighty life force, no one knew, but it was one of those puzzles that would occupy many a delightful morning for Rickie and her family in the years to come. To consider that such a tiny jewel of a creature as the Pine Warbler could play Orpheus' lute to such momentous transformation was always a wonder to her.

When the season ebbed, as it was doing then, the birds worked their way to the shore and followed it southwest to their wintering ground or used it for a jumping off point for their long over-water flights. The shore at this time of year was actually a river of migrating birds and sea creatures.

Nature had laid out a banquet for these travelers. The shoreline was covered in fruits and seeds of every description, while the edge of the sea was packed with small baitfish. Every wave in the ocean was shimmering with tiny menhaden, herring, and silversides. Even the Mole Crabs were looking hearty and robust. It was a time of plenty, but a time of frantic, and in many ways, joyous activity for twitchy travelers, anxious for a quick meal and to be on their way.

Along the dunes and hummocks at the shore, the branches of the black cherry trees hung heavy with purple fruit. Raspberries and blackberries dotted every rock and branch. Currants, grapes, arrow wood drupes, and shadbush all presented their gifts to the travelers, hoping that their offspring would be given a lift and a new home. Rose hips were still going strong and uncountable numbers of white, waxy fruits frosted the bayberry bushes in the dunes. There was even an overabundance of tasty Dragonflies flitting around the dunes, for those birds that were so inclined. It was all there; the pulse and vitality of life at its apex, flowing along the margin of the sea.

In the riverside community there was also an excitement and a sense of urgency. For this was the time when the Riverfolk gathered nuts, collected bayberries for candles, picked fruits for preserves, and stored memories to sustain them through the long winter to come.

These offerings also attracted the attention of the wild creatures; birds of every description flocked to this feast, while striped bass and bluefish tore into the clouds of baitfish along the beach. Nor had this bounty gone unnoticed at the top of the food chain, for the peregrine falcons patrolled the shore looking for a wee songbird that tarried too long at the dinner table, and the harbor seals looked for striped bass that stayed out far past their bedtime at dawn.

There was almost too much of nature's offerings for Rickie and Mr. Rat to choose from. While the black cherries might interest them for pies, and the bayberries for candles, and the pokeweed for dye, Rickie and Rat were after more elusive game: Beach Plums. Beach Plums are sort of the striped bass of the land; elusive, secret, delicious, and jealously guarded, so the competition was fierce for the best.

As they got ready, Rickie and her Father could feel the excitement and urgency of the season. A lunch basket was packed, and they headed for the dock. A few optimistically large gunnysacks were also packed away for the plums. The laneway was stained black with the juice of thousands of black cherries and their pits crunched underfoot.

Rat and his daughter reached the dock, loaded their supplies into the *Beetle*, and carefully made the transition from solid land to the lively catboat. They cranked up the halyards to send the sail clattering up the mast on its hoops, dropped the centerboard, cast off the lines, and were off to the soothing rocking of The River and slap of the northwest chop on the cedar planking. No messing about in the boat today; they were on a mission.

They beached the *Beetle* in a quiet bight behind the beach. Mr. Rat ran the anchor up the sand and planted it firmly above the wrack line. Then he dropped the small kedge anchor off the stern to keep the boat from being grounded by the dropping tide. The *Beetle* gently rocked back and forth swishing her flapping sail before it was dropped and furled. The mud flats and sand bars were dotted with excited shorebirds, taking advantage of the dropping tide to start their breakfast.

"So Dad, why are the shorebirds always traveling and never content to stay in one spot?"

"The mud is always blacker on the other side of the fence."

"Seriously Dad, where do the shorebirds come from, and where do they go? For most of them, we only see them in the spring and fall. Except for the piping plovers, I never see the others nesting."

"No one really knows. It is thought that they go to the arctic in the summer and antipodes in the off season so they have two summers each year and barely see the night sky except in the spring and fall when they need the stars to steer by. A cool crisp day like today must seem downright tropical to them after what they have been through. I have tried to engage them in conversation, to no avail. Unlike your cheeky, loudmouth friend the Bobolink, these fellows are too busy to chat; they have thousands of miles to go."

"How about the Eskimo Curlew? What happened to them? I have never seen one."

"And you probably never will, little one. My grandfather said that when he was young, migrating Curlews would be forced down by late summer gales and take refuge on local beaches and flats. Thousands would dot the shore, but since that time not a single bird has been seen. They had long down-curved bills like a Whimbrel's but about half the size. The Curlews had high-pitched squeaks and whistles. Before alighting, they would circle a field or beach, sometimes hovering, until finding a good spot to land, then glide down to feed on berries or Mole Crabs."

"Mole Crabs? What's the use for Mole Crabs?" asked Rickie.

"There is as you say a 'use' for everything that nature provides, but remember that just because we have no use for one of nature's creations, does not mean it has no place. It is all part of the web of life, and those pesky little Mole Crabs are a great delicacy to the whimbrels, plovers and other shorebirds; it is a fuel source for their long journeys."

"Ick," said Rickie wrinkling her nose.

"Have you ever tried them, shells and all, slowly sautéed with olive oil and garlic? Crunchy like popcorn, mmm."

"Daddddddd…"

Her father laughed and with that they headed into the dunes following a meandering sandy path between fragrant pitch pine trees and sweet fern. As they crested a small dune, Mr. Rat sucked in his breath, grabbed Rickie's shoulder, and put his finger to his lips. Ahead of them a large bayberry bush was a shimmering, jiggling mass of iridescent navy blue.

"Quiet now, be slow and gentle. No extra steps or noise," whispered her father.

"You need to experience this at least once," continued Mr. Rat. "This is one of the greatest gifts that nature has bestowed upon us, or anyone for that matter, at least the ones who are paying attention. Our timing is perfect. Wait until you see what happens next…"

They slowly tiptoed up to the bayberry plant, and then it happened. With a whoosh, the plants lifted up, or so it seemed, as hundreds of birds launched themselves in the air and swirled around them like a dark tornado. Rickie clutched her father's sleeve, but he just laughed and told her to enjoy the show. Everywhere there was the flutter of wings and the soft sibilant voices of swallows. Up they swirled and back down again in a bayberry bush a dozen yards away. As Rickie looked around, she could see similar dark tornadoes the whole length of the beach.

"What is going on?" asked Rickie.

"The Tree Swallows are after the bayberries. Handsome aren't they? Like little penguins, dressed like waiters. They carry the color of Beach Plums on their back and a breaking wave on their tummy, a logical arrangement, unlike that silly Bobolink friend of yours. Impressive, isn't it? Capistrano cannot hold a candle to this."

"Capistrano?"

"The Capistrano Swallows get all the press. They are the egotistical, publicity-hound, prima donna, movie stars of the Swallow world. They get a weeklong fiesta, parades, songs, street fairs, parties, holidays and worldwide coverage. All the children of the town of Capistrano dress in cute little swallow outfits, but the problem is that there are only a handful of Swallows left at Capistrano. I swear those birds must have the world's best press agents.

"But let them have the press," continued Rat. "We have the show. While the paparazzi are fawning over the Capistrano Swallows, following them around, pestering them at every turn, making their lives miserable, we have these Tree Swallows all to ourselves."

"It seems like that is true of most of our local wonders, Dad. The remote, exotic creatures get the glamour, while our local crowd is barely noticed."

"True, true. I have never seen a headline about our Mole Crabs".

"Dad! Seriously now, how about the Bluebird or the Bobolink or even the Luna Moth; they don't get the recognition they deserve."

And it was true. One of the great natural spectacles, the world on the move, was unfolding right in front of them, but no one else even seemed to notice. Certainly not that persnickety little amphibian, thought Rickie, hearing the roar of the *Runabout* as it headed out to sea on a beeline for The Island.

"So true. Take the British birds for instance. My cousin, the famous Water Rat from Cookham Dean on the upper Thames, is always waxing poetical about their English birds, but let's do a quick comparison if you like."

"Yes please," said an eager Rickie.

"Right this way then," answered her father as he snuck up on a red cedar protruding from a dune. "Hear that up-slurred song? Watch carefully for the singer."

Sure enough, a tiny jewel of a bird popped into the open, tilted its head to the sky, and sang its lively song.

Rickie gasped, "It's beautiful. What is it?"

"That, my dear, is the Prairie Warbler. Now take the English Willow Warbler. A fine fellow and attractive compared to the other English birds, but he is a roast beef compared to our Prairie Warbler."[1]

---

1. This is the anglicized version of the French term "rosbif" or "rôti-de-boeuf". Originally this was a derogatory term coined by the French for the British and their cooking, but eventually this barb was adopted by Americans to describe British sailors. In return the British started calling the American sailors "Baked Beans".

"You are being a bird chauvinist, Dad. The poor Willow Warbler would be insulted as would Uncle Rat and his birding colleagues from across the Ocean if they heard that. The British must love their Willow Warbler."

"They do, and they love birding. While the residents of Capistrano are crazy about one bird, the Brits are crazy about all of their birds. I have overstated my case; the willow warbler is not without its charms. Even I have to admit that it has a pleasing song, but in some ways it is a letdown."

"A letdown? How so?" asked Rickie.

Then her father whistled the song of the willow warbler. It was a complex, rippling song with a crescendo in the middle, but then it was drawn out to a faint ending.

"Note how the song droops and runs out of steam at the end. I hate to say it, but…"

"But what?" asked Rickie.

"The Willow Warbler just gets Winded, ha," chortled her father.

"Very pun-y, Dad, but why does he get winded?"

"It is hard to say. Maybe all those Old World worries weigh him down, ha. Maybe those cold summers and warm beer make him depressed. Maybe he gets tired keeping up appearances for all those nosy birders. Compare that to the Prairie Warbler; his song is exuberant and vibrant and optimistic."

"I suppose you are going to mention New World enterprise and vigor, right Dad?" asked Rickie.

"I don't know about that, but one thing is for sure; the Prairie Warbler does not have to keep up appearances for all the birders watching him. I am pretty sure we are the only birders he has seen, or will see. He is a handsome devil, and he knows it. Like your Bobolink, he does not have, ah, any confidence problems."

"That's just ridiculous, you know that Dad, right?" smiled Rickie.

Her father chuckled and gave her a knowing smile.

"Dad, weren't we supposed to be picking Beach Plums?"

"Ah, yes. OK, let's get going"

It was time to get to work, so Ratty led Rickie off to Spyglass Hill. Once on top, they consulted the maps that Rat and his daughter had drawn up in May. Spring seemed so impossibly long ago at the close of this very eventful summer thought Rickie as she remembered her adventures with The Bobolink and the Fireflies and Montaup Hill. From the top of Spyglass Hill, Rickie could see the indigo colors of the ocean on one side and the pastel colors of The River on the other side. Dragonflies, swept down from northern ponds and swamps by the northwest wind the night before, swirled and rattled about the hollows of the dunes; these were big darning needles, Blue Darners and Saddlebag dragonflies. Mr. Rat and his daughter paused to watch a Kestrel dive, grab a Dragonfly in its talons, and fly off to the southwest. Rickie thought she had never seen a hawk as beautiful as the Kestrel.

Then they were off and following the map to what Rat expected would be a bounteous patch of Beach Plums, hoping to get there before Mr. Fox discovered them. As they weaved their way through the dunes, a slow trickle of migrating monarch butterflies passed them; their movements seemed haphazard, but by careful observation, Rickie could see they were headed southwest where all good things arrive from and depart to.

As Rickie and her father crested a hummock, they came upon a rectangular broken wall of decaying bricks, overgrown with raspberries, briars and poison ivy.

"What's this?" asked Rickie.

"It is the remains of one of the Great Houses, which the owners modestly called the Cottages; these luxurious homes used to line the beach. Each one was as grand as Toad Hall, but not grand enough to last."

"What happened to them?"

"The Great Gale took them and everything else, I am afraid. My grandfather told me terrible stories about this storm. It came from the southeast with little warning and carried away all before it. These houses were never rebuilt, for the owners feared another storm, which, thankfully, never came. These foundations are from a bygone, gilded age. Try to imagine dinner being served by waiters with white gloves on the veranda overlooking the sea, followed by waltzes in the ballroom."

"Looks like the only waltzes being done these days are by the mice and raccoons."

They looped around a dune and back toward the pitch pine forest. A small glade opened up before them. Then it was off to another hollow where Rat had staked a claim, at least in his mind, for it was the Wild West out here, and everything was up for grabs. The only chance of success was luck and secrecy. As they descended into a hollow in the dunes, there it was before them: small, gnarled bushes lifting their black fingers through the drifting sand. As Rat and

Rickie got closer, they noticed the branches laden with purple fruit, so much so that some of it had dropped to the ground. Rickie was so excited that she grabbed a gunnysack and dived right in, ignoring the poison ivy and briars. *That girl will need a good scrub tonight*, thought Rat as he cautiously worked his way into the bushes.

"So, Dad, how do the beach plums turn purple? There is nothing purple in the dunes; it is all brown and gray and white with a bit of green here and there, but no purple anywhere. If I mix those colors in my paint set, I would never get purple."

"I have to believe it is some sort of mysterious alchemy. How else can they turn sand and salt and sun into purple fruit? This transformation is something far beyond our understanding, but these plants have figured it out. Things such as this make me feel like we are cavemen with clubs trying to understand a Swiss watch."

Rickie tried one of the plums, careful not to nick a tooth on its large pit.

"Mmmm, so good. I was expecting something salty. Maybe something like the wind off the water. Or even low tide, or bland like a rose hip. But it is not like that at all, is it? It is incredible, distinctive, and exuberant. It is sweet and slightly medicinal, like elderberries. More alchemy?"

"Yup."

One plum after another went into her mouth, staining her hands and lips.

"So Dad, if I eat a lot of beach plums will I be imbued with the strength of the wind and waves?"

"No, but you might turn purple. From the stains on your hands, it looks like you are halfway there. You might want to ease off a point or so on the plums," urged her dad. "We will appreciate them even more in January if we make preserves out of them."

When they had picked their fill, but not too many, for they had to leave some for the wild creatures, Rat and Rickie hefted their gunnysacks for the return trip.

"Before we go, I want to introduce you to an old friend. She is the most secret and treasured of all my discoveries in the dunes."

They took a faint path through a miniature pitch pine forest, twisting this way and that until the path petered out in a briar patch. Around and under the briars they went, pushing their way through thick fragrant, sweet pepper bushes until they came to a small clearing. In the middle of the clearing was the oldest beach plum plant that Rickie had ever seen. There was not a footprint in the sand, not a soul had found her.

"As a child I remember my father showing me this matriarch. It was old even then, but look at her now, elderly but spritely. She survived the Great Gale, ice storms, heat, and drought. And young Water Rats pulling at her branches. Look how she is still throwing fruit."

And sure enough this stately plum had an arm extended and loaded with berries as if asking Mr. Rat for one last dance.

As Mr. Rat explained, "This is a very special plant, and I have a separate bag for her berries. We will gather only a few handfuls, take them home and carefully pit them, crack the shell, and then plant the seeds around the river. I think it is what she wants."

So they hauled their gunnysacks to the faithful *Beetle* and left, having harvested much more than just plums.

Chapter 16

The Counting Day

"Success is counted sweetest
by those who ne'er succeed.
To comprehend a nectar
Requires the sorest need."
  ℱ Emily Dickinson, "Success is counted sweetest", 1859

"…happiness is not found in things you possess, but in
what you have the courage to release…"
  ℱ Nathaniel Hawthorne

The Counting Day for the Scavenger Hunt had finally arrived, and the children gathered on the croquet grounds of The Inn to present their treasures and await the final tally.

The Leader Board had been set up, and it had entries for those youngsters who had already submitted their solutions to the judges. Most of the experienced young animals had not submitted any finds, preferring to keep their discoveries secret, and not give their competitors an edge. The newbies had already entered what they had found, and the Leader Board clearly showed the Chipmunks in the lead with 70 points, with a young Weasel at 65 points not far behind. This was a sizeable lead, but many of the other contestants felt they had a chance if their solutions were correct.

"Alright, let's get started," said Mrs. Badger with a smile. "We all know the answer to the first question, right?

*"With this the author can write
And so too the birds take flight."*

"Chirpy said it was a quill, which is possible, but you can only write with a quill. The actual answer is a feather since you can write and fly with a feather."

"So let's get down to business. Here is the next puzzle, the Smack-it riddle:

*"It wears golden bands and rhymes with racket,
which is what you'll make, if you smack it."*

"Please bring your treasures up to the awards table in a paper bag with your name on it."

Toady, Portly, and Mr. Beaver's son, Buck, brought their bags up to the counting table and the judging committee looked inside.

Mrs. Badger, wise to the way of young tricksters, was careful to listen to Toady's bag before opening it, and, sure enough, she heard a buzz.

Mrs. Badger shot him a stern look, "Toady, what have you done?"

Toady giggled, but Mrs. Badger did not open the bag; she simply asked Toady what was in the bag.

He responded, "A Yellow Jacket, a live one."

"The correct answer is indeed Yellow Jacket. 15 points to Portly, and Buck, and, ahem, Toady. Now for the next riddle:"

*"He has lost his twinkle and cannot shine.
For from the heavens he has fallen
To live forever in the salt and brine.
On five points you can find him crawlin'."*

On this almost all the children brought little bags up to the counting table.

"Well, well I see that this riddle was too easy. The answer, of course, is a Starfish. 10 Points for these happy scavengers.

"For 15 points, here is the next riddle:"

*"A yellow gal named Sue, looks to the sky
And follows the sun with her raccoon eye."*

106

Only Rickie and Chirpy submitted answers.

"I guess that was a little tough. The answer is a Black-eyed Susan flower."

"The next one might be the hardest riddle of all. For 30 points:"

"Twisting, turning, climbing to the dawn
Its green fingers lift a velvet bluish horn."

There were a lot of nervous glances; nobody seemed to have solved this riddle until Rickie stood up and proudly trotted to the judging stand to the oohs and aahs of the audience. Mrs. Badger opened that bag and smiled; Rickie had solved the puzzle.

"30 Points to Miss Rickie for solving this riddle. The answer is a Morning Glory. That gives her 55 points, as you can see on the Leader Board. She is closing in on the Chipmunks."

"OK, next clue: For 10 points, were you able to solve this?"

"His name is big as you will see, but he is as small as he can be
For in the brine he wants to be, to dart and wiggle in the sea.
On some ice he lays in rows, served with radish from a horse,
Pink and yummy there he goes, get you ready for the first course."

Most of the contestants brought up a bag for this item and the judging committee went through each one and updated the Leader Board.

"Well it looks like most of you got this at least partially right. The answer is Jumbo Shrimp. If you submitted a skimpy Shrimp, you only get 5 points."

"Our next riddle is rather tricky to decipher and trickier to find. For 30 points:"

"With this money there is nothing that you can buy,
For it will slip through your fingers if you try."

Only Toady, Portly, and a Weasel submitted an entry.

"The answer to this riddle is: A Sand Dollar. All three got the name right, but only Toady was able to produce a real Sand Dollar and thus gets the full 30 points. As you can see from the tally on the board, Toady has a total of 65 points and is closing in on the leaders."

"The next riddle is simple when you know the answer, but it seems to have stumped almost everyone. For 30 points:"

"With bricks and mortar he is bold
But jams and jellies it can hold."

There was only one child that submitted a bag for this, a rather smug Portly.

"It looks like Portly got it, a Mason Jar! This puts Portly in the lead with 95 points! Is there anyone out there who can challenge him?"

"For 10 points, do you have the following? Remember we need an exact match, and it has to be handled with care."

"On his back this plodding fellow carries his house,
You can find him at eye-level for the art-loving mouse"

Most of the children had some entry for this, but it was not a Hermit Crab and a Turtle was not specific enough. The correct answer was a Painted Turtle.

"So I see that a few of you were able to find painted turtles. As we can see, Rickie at 70 is second to Toady. Can she pull into the lead? For 10 points, did you find this?"

"Spires of gold reaching upward you might see
But it has no value unless you are a bee."

The botanically minded children, including Rickie, submitted items to the judging table.

"It looks like Rickie and some others were able to come up with the right answer, a Goldenrod flower."

"We are down to our last question. Toady is still in the lead, with 95 points, but Rickie is catching up with 80 points. The last puzzle will decide who wins the first prize. For 30 points:"

"Sheds water so you will not sink
But on its pages you can write with ink"

There was a lot of murmuring and looking around. Rickie looked at Toady and Toady looked at Rickie; it was a bit of a standoff. Toady was wearing an inscrutable, conflicted expression on his face, both excited and frustrated. He went to get up and head to the judging table, but then sat down.

Rickie saw this and shot right up. She quickly scampered up to the table and presented her treasure. The judges opened it up and Mrs. Badger looked at Toady and asked if he had also solved the riddle, but Toady stayed glued to his seat and silent. Then Mrs. Badger made the pronouncement.

"The answer is: Birch Bark. The winner of this year's scavenger hunt is ... Rickie!"

Uproar ensued as the children cheered and hooted. Rickie jumped up and ran to the stage to examine her new canoe, but she noticed Toady still in his seat looking at her with a puzzled, imploring expression. Rickie kept an eye on her rival after the contest broke up and noticed the litterbug throwing a paper bag into a clump of bushes. After everyone left, she retrieved the bag and was perplexed to find a piece of birch bark inside. Toady could have won the contest; why didn't he?

Maybe he was not as selfish as she had assumed.

On the birch bark was etched the image of a bird that Rickie did not recognize; it was an odd grouse-like bird with peculiar "ears" and a highly animated expression. Surely Toady had dreamed up such a ridiculous bird, but Rickie made a note to herself to check her reference books and see if such a bird existed.

Later that day Rickie pawed through her bird identification guides. What she found astounded her. Had she misjudged Toady? How could an uncouth twerp such as Toady know of such an esoteric bird as the Heath Hen? Maybe there was more to this little amphibian than she had realized.

❖ Chapter 17 ❖
Omens & Portents

"As fair art thou, my bonnie lass,
So deep in luve am I:
And I will luve thee still, my dear,
Till a' the seas gang dry:"
ℰ Robert Burns, A Red, Red Rose, 1794

Summer had expended itself, but the gray thoughts of the season to follow had barely started to creep into Mr. Rat's consciousness. Soon enough it would be time to haul out the *Beetle*, stack wood, hang storm windows, can fruit, and do all the other usual tasks to get ready for winter, but for now Mr. Rat intended to enjoy Summer's gentle afterglow. It was too early for the melancholy thoughts of fall to drag him down, for there were still the glorious September days on the water, or so he thought.

On this fateful day Ratty woke to a crunching and thudding of heavy surf from the Ocean side. He could hear the grinding sound of retreating waves clawing the sand back to the sea whence it came and the thump of new rollers climbing over the shoulders of the previous waves.

Expecting to find a storm in progress, Mr. Rat stepped outside to investigate but was surprised to find a light southeast breeze barely riffling the water. The air was misty and redolent with the smell of salt and ground up seaweed, but Rat's sensitive nose picked up something more. It was a wafting of warm, tropical vapors from the sea, a scent so out of place in New England that he started to have some troubling thoughts about the day.

There is something very peculiar happening, thought Mr. Rat, *very peculiar indeed.* Rat's animal instinct could sense trouble, and his natural curiosity led him to investigate.

Ambling down to the shore, Rat noticed that the farm animals seemed jumpy and nervous. None of the songbirds said their usual hellos this morning, and few were to be seen. These cheerful sprites were seldom silent; Mr. Rat wondered what had spooked them.

Mr. Rat was startled to see Chimney Swifts flying close to the ground; usually they were so high up that they were just tiny black silhouettes against the sky, but now they acted as if they were wary of their usual lofty station. What was up there that would scare them?

When Mr. Rat reached the shore, he was interested to see huge swells running up the beach and was concerned for the inexperienced boaters who might try to weather such a sea. There was a leaden feel to the air, as if a weight pressed down on him, and the air was unnaturally warm, almost languid, for an autumn day.

High clouds raced overhead at an unnatural speed. Ratty saw masses of white water frosting all the offshore reefs, promising good fishing; the Striped Bass loved nothing so much as a good romp in the surf.

Mr. Rat trotted over to Mole's burrow and barged right in.

"Moley," said Rat, rousting him from his bed. "There is something peculiar about the ocean today..."

"There's something even more exciting going on inside my eyelids..." replied Mole as he rolled over.

Rat prodded Moley again, "But we must investigate it. Shake out a reef and get going. Fetch the gear and some biscuits; no time for breakfast."

As Rat and Mole set out for the Ocean in the *Beetle*, they tried to make sense of what they encountered. The air barely filled their sail, yet the waves continued to build on the beach. Rat was surprised to see rafts of open ocean birds seemingly exhausted and bedraggled resting on The River. Why were these pelagic birds here on The River instead of out to sea? Why were they exhausted and battered? No matter why these pelagics are here, Rickie will be excited to see them, thought Rat with a smile.

The sky took on a peculiar burnished yellow color; what could cause that thought Mr. Rat. Forest fires? Dust in the air? Had the sun given up and decided to set early today? It did not make sense.

Of all the unusual omens that Mr. Rat observed this morning, it was the tide that troubled him the most. It seemed to be lower than he had ever remembered it; it was as if the plug had been pulled on the Ocean. *Where has the water gone, and why?* thought Mr. Rat. He expressed his concerns to Mr. Mole, but Mole paid it no heed, excited to be on the water for what promised to be a thrilling fishing trip. But the issue of the tide nagged and pulled at Rat's subconscious; instinctually he sensed danger, even if he could not quite put a finger on it. Certainly being on the Ocean with a heavy surf was dangerous enough, but there was something more sinister in the offing.

Oddly enough, there was a certain gaiety in the air among the other Riverfolk; the newly-exposed sand bars gave the locals a welcome opportunity to dig clams from previously-inaccessible flats. The exceptionally low tide was a gift from Neptune that they were eager to avail themselves of; however, Neptune's offerings are not to be taken lightly. He would expect repayment, and his price was usually steep.

The shorebirds also took note of the tide and noisily flocked to the new mudflats. All this activity had not gone unnoticed by Rickie, and she eagerly set out in her new canoe for one of the sandbars that were speckled with spritely shorebirds. Rickie was excited and perplexed to see such open ocean birds as dovekies, shearwaters, and petrels on the river. Most peculiar of all was a Great Northern Diver, a Loon that seemed to follow the canoe.

Rickie beached the canoe on a new sand bar and fished out her binoculars and notepad. The Loon began yodeling and Rickie could make out these oddly mournful words:

I hold the soul of a forsaken Cree,
The Ancients sent me here to help you flee.

These were curious things to say on such a fine day thought Rickie, as she walked along the sand looking for shorebirds. She could feel the thump of the heavy surf on the far side of the barrier beach, but she felt safe here in The River on her freshly minted island. An unusual shorebird, which looked like a small Whimbrel, passed overhead calling plaintively. A shock of recognition left Rickie thunderstruck. It certainly looked the part, but could it really be an Eskimo Curlew? It seemed to be trying to draw her off the sand bar. It wheeled and turned and wheeled again around her as if to warn her of some hidden danger.

Rat and Mole traveled out The River onto The Ocean, and what a terrifyingly magnificent sight greeted them. Clouds of mist and salt spray drifted in off the sea. All the reefs that were formally hidden now wore foaming crests of white. With mounting excitement, Ratty even spotted a new reef that was not on the charts. Was this another of Mr. Fox's secret spots? On a number of nights Rat had watched Fox in this general area. What could be more perfect than a secret unmarked reef?

He turned the boat toward the foundling reef to investigate, but, before he did, he noticed something that made the hackles stand up on the back of his neck.

"Why look at that Mole, the Kerberos Ledge is exposed!"

There it was, a brooding, sullen hulk, black and alien. It had dripping twisted Medusa locks of writhing seaweed upon its brow. The two animals stared in awe and terror; they had never seen The Kerberos in the air before. This reef did not belong to the world of sun and spray and birds and animals. It was the haunt of crabs and eels and all the other dark slimy horrors of the deep. A gentle breeze had never caressed its brow, nor had the sun shined upon its sullen cheek. For decades it had laid hidden and waiting, but now it had emerged to look for new victims for its insatiable maw and, maybe, thought Rat, release the demons from the underworld. Then Rat remembered what he had heard on Montaup Hill about the coming darkness and gave a shudder.

There was something else nagging at Rat, some long-forgotten memory. The surf, the birds, Kerberos, the tide, what was it? Something terrible was about to happen, but what? Then an old memory came back to him; when he was child, his grandfather told him about an exceptionally low tide so many years ago and what it presaged.

It struck Rat like a thunderclap! His eyes wide in terror, he turned to Mole and began to yell like he had never yelled in his life.

"NOW MOLE, NOW. WE MUST FLEE!"

❧ Chapter 18 ❧
The River Styx

"And do you wait a moment, you husky-noised sea;
For somewhere I believe I heard my mate responding to me,
So faint--I must be still, be still to listen!...
Do not be decoyed elsewhere!
That is the whistle of the wind--it is not my voice
That is the fluttering, the fluttering of the spray."
ƒ Walt Whitman, *Out of the Cradle Endlessly Rocking*, 1859

Rat was in a fury and yelled at Mole to get underway. Mole was reeling in a large striped bass and was in no mood to leave. In a rage, Mr. Rat took a knife from his belt and cut Mole's line. Mole was concerned; he had never seen the usually unflappable Mr. Rat this worked up, but when Mr. Rat explained to him what the low water meant, he too was gripped by a deathly terror.

As they worked their way to the dock, they desperately flagged down young Toady and Portly on The *Runabout*, explaining the situation. Toady and Portly zoomed off to spread the word. Next Mr. Rat told the Harbormaster and the Shellfish Warden, both of whom fanned out along the shore urging the residents to secure their boats and get to shore. Riverfolk who were digging clams on newly exposed flats were warned, and hastily returned to the high ground on the Riverbank. Rat tied up the *Beetle* to the dock as securely as he could and made best speed to fetch the Constable as Mole ran out to the beach to evacuate the residents.

Mr. Rat felt certain there was a storm coming, a terrible gale, a hurricane in fact. He suspected that the excessively low tide was the hurricane pulling up water before it flooded their community with a storm surge. While Mr. Rat was greatly respected along the waterfront, there was barely a breath of wind, and some folk had their doubts; they were lackadaisical about securing their boats and homes on such a fine day.

These doubts started to fade as the wind picked up and intermittent sheets of rain lashed their faces. Fueled with a new urgency, they redoubled their efforts, trying to stave off panic. Loose items were tied down or stowed in cellars, farm animals were herded inside, and windows were hastily boarded up. Word was beginning to spread and the bell in the church steeple began to toll.

The wind was building and began sweeping over the dunes, driving clouds of Tree Swallows like falling leaves before an October squall. The sand, so soft and gentle in the summer, was turned into stinging nettles as it pelted those still on the beach. The air was full of flying projectiles. At first it was light debris and even laundry left out on the line, but as the storm progressed, heavier objects became airborne. Shingles were stripped off roofs and sent spinning downwind. Branches were snapped off trees and became airborne.

Conditions were degenerating quickly on the water. Frightened Riverfolk worked to secure their boats as sails were unclipped from masts, hatches were reinforced, and extra lines were set up. The boatyard was pulling boats as fast as they could. The Concordia was already out, for Badger had been watching the barometer and instinctually knew something momentous was afoot, but there was no time for most of the other boats.

Toady and Portly had the fastest boat on the water and for once the scream of its engine was a welcome sound. They raced around The River spreading the word and ferrying frightened animals to shore.

A preoccupied Rickie was still on an exposed sandbar in the River counting shorebirds. The Loon continued to sing:

Neptune is not one to proffer an easy gift,
For the unwary his retribution will be swift.

On this strand no mortal lingers,
Lest you be caught by his cold, gray fingers.
Be lively; your footsteps must be light,
or you will feel The Ocean's terrible might.

Young Rickie suddenly noticed water lapping at her ankles. She could see a change in the weather and decided to head back. But when Rickie looked up the sandbar, she realized to her horror that The Canoe was gone, taken by the rising waters. In her excitement, she had forgotten to set the anchor. The water was rising fast and starting to tug at her legs. Rickie was surrounded by roiling gray seawater and trapped on the flooding island. She could no longer see the shore in the gathering murk and lost all sense of direction. She was alone, utterly alone, as the world closed in on her. The rising water started to creep higher up her legs, and she struggled to remain upright as floating debris began hitting her. The wind whistled in her ears. In a panic she waved and screamed, but no one saw her on the lonely, flooding sand spit.

As the weather thickened, flares could be seen shooting up through the murk. Toady would deftly zoom over to the distressed mariners, lift them from their boat and ferry them safely to shore only to see another flare or hear a desperate horn. The *Runabout* was getting dinged and smacked around by the debris in the water, but Toady hardly noticed.

Ashore, Rat, Otter, Toad, and others from town were on the high ground of The Point anxiously scanning the gray waves of the now threatening River. Rat was gravely concerned after finding out that Rickie had last been seen in The Canoe. Mr. Rat had a horrible premonition that she was out on one of the newly exposed sand bars. Panic gripped Mr. Rat when he saw The Canoe drift by the Point without Rickie in it. He was poised to take the *Beetle* out to look for her, but Badger grabbed Rat in his iron grip and sadly shook his head.

"Ratty, old friend, I cannot let you go out there. You would never get back."

Rat relented and anxiously continued to watch, hoping against hope that his daughter had made it to shore. Otter and Old Toad were also concerned because the *Runabout* was no longer visible.

The wind came in shrieking gusts, driving the rain horizontally into the faces of the worried watchers. Bits of spume, torn from the waves, could be seen flying up over the dunes. Trees bent over and creaked. Leaves were flayed from their branches and plastered on the windward side of houses. The big window in the Cole's house was stoved in. Oaks started to lose their limbs with reports like rifle shots. Their branches hit the ground with a thump and made the watchers wince. A derelict boat, which had parted its cable, drifted by the Point. Next a roof went floating up river. The big white pine at Oleg's house keeled over, crunching his boathouse roof, and its roots ripped out a twenty-foot disk of dripping earth. The tolling of the church bell stopped followed by a horrible rending crash as the steeple toppled over and exploded into a pile of splintered timbers.

Meanwhile on the water Toady and Portly had done all they could and were worried about The *Runabout*; it was not built for heavy weather and was shipping too much water. It was time to head back; their work was done. So they turned, put the storm to their back, and surfed toward home on a following sea. The gray, opaque River was full of trees, spars, decking, and other debris, so they had to carefully thread their way through the slop. As Toady deftly guided the nimble *Runabout* among the jostling and grinding flotsam, Otter frantically bailed. The spray and rain stung their faces and blurred their vision as the two fought against the onslaught.

Their friendly River had turned into the River Styx, the path to the underworld. As they passed the Indian shell middens, Toady thought he could hear a voice above the screeching furies of the storm. In and out it faded as Toady strained to listen. Then it came to him, sharp and insistent. Toady suddenly froze in terror, the worst dread he had ever felt. The storm was dangerous and terrifying but this was much worse; it was something forgotten, something left behind, some tragedy about to happen. It called to him from the depths of his soul. He grabbed Portly by the shoulder as he heard these words:

Gather your courage; you must turn and face the storm,
For you are the guardian of generations yet unborn.
Emptiness will haunt your soul if you do not try,

Find the strength and seek out her plaintive cry.
Heed the words thus spoken,
Or forever more will your heart be broken.

Toady convinced the scared and reluctant Portly that they must go back one more time and so they pointed the little craft into the wind and headed down river.

The vigil continued at The Point as Ratty's despair grew with every passing minute. Boathouses along the River were undermined and started to slump into the water like elephants kneeling down. Other houses were lifted off their foundations and floated upstream. By now the River was a turbid slurry of debris, grinding and crunching and slamming up river before the wind, but worse was to come, much worse.

The ever alert Badger was the first to notice it. A solid black line had formed on the horizon, and he watched in horror as it loomed out of the gray mist.

"IT'S THE STORM SURGE," shouted Badger at the looming menace. The line resolved itself into three huge, black waves.

These walls of destruction were headed their way. Nothing could survive such an onslaught; homes and boats or even the dunes of the beach would be swept away. Rickie, wherever she was, and the *Runabout* were doomed if they were caught by the storm surge. Ratty, Otter, Toad, and Badger screamed in despair; all was certainly lost.

But then it happened. Ratty heard it first, the re-assuring throaty roar of the *Runabout's* V-12 engine. He perked up and pointed upriver. He yelled in Mr. Toad's ear that he thought he heard the engine. It was getting louder, and then Toad and Otter could hear it also as everyone strained to peer through the murk as rain stung their eyes. Then the *Runabout's* outline hove into view as the brave boat plunged through the chop and struggled to get to The Point with the tidal wave of the storm surge only minutes behind it.

But it was not to be; there came the crunch of rending mahogany as the craft hit a submerged piling. The mighty engine coughed and gave its final gasp. The *Runabout* was reduced to a swamped hulk drifting by The Point. As the boat got closer, Rat and his friends could see that its bow was stoved in, and it was taking on water; however, Mr. Rat leapt for joy when he saw three small heads peering over the shattered windscreen.

"Quick, a line. Lend a hand!" Yelled Mr. Rat.

Badger, prepared as usual, produced a stout length of manila, which Ratty secured to a piling and ran to the water. With one mighty, desperate heave, Rat threw the line to the *Runabout*.

The heavy line was caught by the nimble Portly, and he handed the sharp end to Toady. Toady slipped the rope under Rickie's arms and with a quick flick and twist of the wrist he tied The Knot. Toady wrapped one arm around Rickie's slender waist, and they all clasped the scratchy line in a deathly grip as the doomed *Runabout* was swept out from under them. Into the water they went, desperately holding the rope as they were hit again and again by floating debris. The line went taut and vibrated as it swung them in the current. There was great yelling and screaming from the shore as everyone pitched in to haul the three terrified animals ashore. Neptune only reluctantly released his captives, but slowly the vibrating, dripping line was pulled in. As the youngsters got within reach, Badger grabbed them in his mighty grip and handed them off to the others to carry to higher ground.

Leadership was a quality that Mrs. Badger possessed in great abundance, and never more so than in a crisis. Today was the worst crisis that this generation of Riverfolk had ever experienced, and Mrs. Badger rose to the occasion. She had commandeered The Inn at the Point and set up a field hospital. The pale and limp animals were carried up to The Inn and handed to Mrs. Badger.

"Oh the poor dears," gasped Mrs. Badger as each dripping youngster was brought in.

Mrs. Badger forgot the salting of her rose garden, the muddy tracks across her carpet, the Mole Crabs, and Toady's feisty Yellow Jacket. All was forgiven; she was beginning to see Toady in a new light.

The three young animals were toweled dry, given fresh clothes (comically big on their small frames), and wrapped in blankets. They were placed around The Inn's great fireplace, their faces illuminated by its glow, while Mrs. Badger heated up the stove. Rickie's eyes were red from the ocean's salt and her tears, as her thankful father hugged her.

The shaken little creatures shivered around the fire, but presently, Mrs. Badger's hot chocolate coursed through their bodies bringing warmth and life to their extremities. Gradually they could unclench their fingers. Mrs. Badger set to work applying balm and wrappings to their raw paws, scraped and abraded from the rope. Rickie's fur began to dry and fluff, Portly's eyes regained their mischievous twinkle, and a healthy green glow returned to Toady's face. The three little creatures did not notice the crashing, snapping tumult outside the heavy fieldstone walls of the Inn or the storm surge sloshing by The Point, or the wind trying to lift the roof or the salt spray ratcheting the windows like birdshot. They were safe and secure in this granite redoubt surrounded by their loving family and friends.

Brenda the innkeeper produced a bottle for the parents and apologized, "It is not a very good port, but it is the best I can do."

"Any port in a storm!" responded Otter, but few laughed.

As the youngsters sat around the fire, a silky sleepiness crept up on little cat paws, and they began to slump. Rickie looked over at her little rescuer with half-lidded eyes, and for the first time in her life, but certainly not the last, she smiled at him. The Mole Crab Incident and his other outrages, large and small, were finally forgiven. The three drifted off into a dreamless sleep, only to awake the next day in their own warm, snug beds, not knowing or caring how they got there.

Soon enough the eye of the great gale passed, and the wind backed around to the northwest. Its cold airs ripped the tops off the incoming swells and threw them back, like the white manes of Poseidon's charging horsemen sent to dash themselves upon the ravaged shore.

The battered hulk of the *Runabout* drifted up river only to be pinned against the pilings of the bridge and crushed. Its bright new supercharged Italian V-12 sank to the bottom, to begin a second life.

Young Toady had finally destroyed Mr. Toad's beloved *Runabout*, and Old Toad could not have been more proud of him.

 The End

Epilogue

The next morning the Riverfolk were greeted by a scene of utter devastation. There was a wrack line of smashed timbers lining The River. Derelict houses were seen awash in the river or stranded on the shore. The community was totally isolated; all the roads were washed out and telegraph poles were down. The Town was full of uprooted trees and crushed buildings.

In time the damage to the river community would be repaired. Within a week, those surviving trees such as the dogwoods, apples, and shadbush that lost their leaves, confused about the season, re-flowered and heartened the Riverfolk with their spring colors. Exotic tropical migrating birds such as warblers and tanagers that had been swept north with the storm alighted on their branches and sang a song of thanks.

Unlike the Great Gale, no one would starve this time, thanks to the generosity of Mr. Toad, nor would anyone face the winter without lodgings, for those animals that lost their homes were invited to stay at The Inn or Toad Hall while their homes were rebuilt.

All the animals pitched in as best they could. Beaver and his son Buck were kept busy clearing downed trees and making carpentry repairs. Otter and Portly worked along the waterfront. Mr. Toad was busy dawn to dusk helping the needy while his son lent his carpentry and mechanical skills to those animals whose homes were damaged or lost.

The *Beetle* and many other boats were found in fields and yards, stranded by the high water. They were put on rollers and gently nudged back into an apologetic River. Mr. Fox's *Ghost* and a few other boats successfully rode out the storm on their moorings because Toady was able to warn their owners to drop extra lines.

Everywhere there was a bustle of activity to recover from the hurricane. Sunken boats in the harbor were refloated. Roofs were replaced and walls repaired. Cabins that floated upriver were towed downriver, put on rollers, and winched back to their foundations. Burrows were pumped out. Trees were replanted and gardens re-sown. The River was surveyed and new markers were placed.

Kerberos returned to his dark watery realm.

Toady's standing in the community made a radical shift for the better on that fateful day. Whereas before the storm, parents would shun him, now Toady was welcomed as a hero wherever he went. In his previous life, Toady would have puffed up with pride, but now he accepted the accolades with a bit more humility than was typical of the Toad line. Mr. Toad beamed whenever his son's name was mentioned, and he was already working on some wildly exaggerated stories about Toady's exploits.

Among the wreckage and chaos, Toady made the discovery that would forever change the course of Riverfront history. He found a shadbush near The River that had been stripped of leaves, but still bearing one precious fruit: Rickie's Canoe. The Canoe was tangled up in the shadbush, but with a little help from Buck, Toady was able to carefully extricate it and assess the damage. They quietly brought The Canoe to the Boatyard for repairs. For the next few days, Toady and Buck worked feverishly in secret restoring the little treasure. The snapped ribs were replaced, as was a sprung thwart. New birch bark replaced the torn sections and warm spruce gum was used to seal the seams. On the bow of the canoe, Toady etched, in the Malecite Indian tradition, a Catamount into the new birch bark on the starboard side, and a Heath Hen on the larboard side, signifying the bravery and confidence of the bird.

By the third night the work was done. Toady carried The Canoe out of the workshop, quietly deposited it by the door of the Rat family burrow, and silently slipped away. As his dad had advised him, this gift required discretion and subtlety, not something that Toady was particularly good at. So going against his instinct, Toad included no boasting or bragging note with The Canoe, nothing at all except a small 'T' that he engraved on the new thwart. As his father explained, Rickie dearly loved puzzles and would eventually figure it out.

Days went by as Toady waited on pins and needles. Then one morning, a beaming Mr. Toad came into his son's room holding a letter addressed, in a delicate hand, to Master Toady, Esq., Toadmoor Acres. Toady nervously opened the letter and read the calligraphy. It was an invitation from Rickie, asking if he would like to take a picnic cruise on the *Beetle*!

Now it was Rickie's turn to wait on pins and needles, for Mr. Toad made Toady wait a couple of days and pen a careful response. Sending the letter to Toady was an audacious move on Rickie's part, but it was a new world these days in which young ladies did such bold things. Rickie considered herself independent and above such worries, but she was still concerned that Toady would decline her invitation. Of course, such worries were unfounded, for there was nothing that Toady wanted more than that trip with Rickie. He sent her a reply and a date was arranged.

On the appointed day Toady made a detour to Mrs. Badger's, shyly knocking on her door. She seemed surprised, but not unpleased, to see the young Toad.

"To what do I owe the pleasure, my young master?" asked a cheerful Mrs. Badger.

"I would like some flowers for a friend," said an uncharacteristically subdued and shy Toady.

Mrs. Badger looked puzzled for a few seconds and then a broad smile creased her face.

"Ah, very good! I know just the thing for the wee lass. Hold on for a second or two."

Shortly thereafter, a beaming Mrs. Badger returned with a bouquet of blazing star flowers and a grateful Toady left holding his treasure. By this time Mr. Badger had roused himself from the breakfast table to investigate the commotion. When he saw Toady leave with the flowers, he nodded his approval and his gruff continence softened. Then his wife turned to him with soft, glowing eyes.

"Do you remember the first flowers you gave me?" she said to Mr. Badger as she walked over to him, took his paws in hers, and tenderly looked up at him...

Toady arrived early at the dock and nervously paced up and down. As he waited for Rickie, he admired the diving terns, the waves gently careening through the pilings, the sun scintillating off the water, and the soft breeze from the southwest. Suddenly all these river delights evaporated and his world contracted around the small figure staggering toward him. It was Rickie, dressed in her best pinafore, wrestling an impossibly large picnic basket.

As Rickie stepped in the *Beetle*, it sank a tiny fraction of an inch and the displaced water raised the level of The River an even tinier fraction of an inch. It was not enough for you or me to notice, but The River noticed, and she put on her most benevolent airs as the two animals set out upon her waters. As the *Beetle* sailed toward the beach, the two animals could see their future ahead of them in the smooth water of The River and their tumultuous past trailing out behind them in the *Beetle's* gurgling wake.

Although the two youngsters were nervous and awkward, they were able to make it to the beach that day. As the keel scrunched on the sand, Toady nimbly hopped out of the *Beetle* and planted the anchor firmly up on the beach. He trotted back to the boat and extended his hand to help Rickie step out of the boat. She took the proffered hand, stepped out, and turned pink when she realized what she had done.

After enjoying Rickie's carefully prepared picnic, they set sail back to the dock. Toady scampered out of the *Beetle*, secured the lines, and extended a hand to Rickie. This time there was no pink to be seen when she took his hand, just a soft smile.

After the gear had been stowed, Rickie turned to Toady and said, "I sure had a good time today."

She nervously looked at him, expecting a response.

"Sure, yes, it was fun…" added Toady awkwardly.

"I do enjoy being on The River," added Rickie nervously.

The oblivious Toady, quickly added, "So do I."

Rickie's eyes were darting to his face, hoping he would say the hard word but he did not seem to get the message and the two just stared at each other in silence.

Toad was initially mystified, but finally figured it out and said, "Yes it was lovely; I would like to go out again … that is, if you want to…"

"I would," said a beaming Rickie.

"Tomorrow?"

"Yes!"

And so it began. The next trip was more relaxed, and so was the next. Eventually they became fixtures on The River with Rickie, or even Toady, at the helm. A lot of things changed for Toady that Fall. Toady learned to appreciate the subtler things in life, not just the charm of a boat under sail.

By late fall, as Rickie knew it would, Orion had returned to his station, and the industrious riverside community was patched up as best it could be. By March, the shadbush bloomed, and it signaled the return of the Timberdoodle; Rickie and Toady enjoyed watching the Woodcock's dance at dusk and strained to hear more of the prophecy that Rickie first heard on Montaup Hill. They were never sure if it was The Protector's voice or just the playing of the wind in the cattail reeds, but they heard something.

By the next season the hurricane damage had been repaired, but The *Runabout's* mighty engine remained at the bottom of The River. Was it content there? In general it was thought that the former terror of the river was enjoying its placid retirement. Even today you can see the great beast with its swaying green tresses of seaweed placidly holding court in the clear lipid waters of The River.

On many outings Rickie and Toady would sail by the engine to say hello and realize how far they had come. Toady considered how many miles that engine had taken him only to realize that his home was right here on The River with Rickie. Toady had finally found his anchor.

Appendix
& Natural History Notes

Amundsen and the South Pole: Of all of Mr. Toad's stories, this is the one that got him in the most trouble. Before Amundsen's conquest of the South Pole, various teams had attempted the North Pole, and at the time there was a raging controversy about who was first. Amundsen wanted to avoid such a problem and was meticulous about documenting and marking the South Pole when he got here. Because of this, he was very upset when he heard of Toad's story about him. It blew up into an international incident and Mr. Rat had to call in some favors from his friend, Fridtjof Nansen to smooth out the ruffled feathers.

Banshee: The banshee is a female spirit in Irish mythology that heralds, via a horrible screeching and keening, a coming death of a family member. Many of the residents of the riverfront were from the Wee Island of Hibernia so Banshees were occasionally heard.

Barometer 27: During one of his sessions at the Inn, Mr. Toad claimed to have saved his crew during a storm that was so intense the barometer was at 27 and falling. Only a true hero such as Mr. Toad could survived such gale; Carl Cutler writes in *Greyhounds of the Sea: The Story of the American Clipper Ship* of many terrible storms, and none pushed the glass below 27. In one harrowing account the clipper ship the *Red Gauntlet* was stuck in a hurricane that lasted 56 hours. The barometer hit 27.5 and the ship was left a floating hulk.

Beach Plums: These fruit-bearing bushes are closely related to cherries. Do not confuse them with rose hips which are common, orange-fruited, prickly bushes; beach plumbs are rare and have no thorns, but you will probably have to brave poison ivy, vicious cat briars, and mosquitoes if you are lucky enough to find a real beach plum bush.

Bobolink: Bobolinks used to be common in New England, but changing land use patterns, early mowing of fields in particular, have endangered this wondrous bird.

If you want to converse with a Bobolink, contact your local Audubon center. The biggest concentration of Bobolinks in my area is in the warm season grassland near Allens Pond in South Dartmouth Massachusetts. A few can even be seen while enjoying lunch at the Bayside Restaurant in Westport. Bobolinks can also be found on private land such as some fields in Little Compton, Rhode Island. A few years ago I was delighted to find them at the Greenvale Winery in Portsmouth, Rhode Island. The key to encountering bobolinks is finding fields that are mowed late.

The Canals of Mars: A blurry image in an inferior telescope can give free reign to a wild imagination and wishful thinking. Such was the case with Percival Lowell when he published intricate drawings of the canals on Mars in books such as *Mars and Its Canals* (1906). Subsequent observations and photographs with better telescopes such as the sixty-inch Mount Wilson Observatory failed to find any canals, but this did not discourage Mr. Toad.

Catamount: The New England name for the Eastern Mountain Lion. Mountain lions used to roam the whole North American continent, but they were thought to have disappeared from New England centuries ago; however, there have been persistent and credible reports of big cats in New England for the last hundred years.

Carbonated Swamp Warbler: You will not find this bird in your bird guides, but it may have existed in extremely small numbers. This is the name of a bird that Audubon painted, but it has never been seen since (except for one mysterious sighting in a cedar swamp in New Jersey about 30 years ago). Most ornithologists consider it cryptozoological, i.e. like Big Foot or mermaids, but the Riverfolk swear they can still find it in their big cedar swamp.

Common Loon: Although loons nest in northern lakes during the summer, I usually find a few on the ocean (off Horseneck Beach in Westport, Massachusetts) in the spring, fall, and even summer. These summer loons are commonly thought to be immature birds. As far as the loon's call, John McPhee had this to say in his delightful book, *The Survival of the Bark Canoe*: "The Crees believed that it was the cry of a dead warrior denied entrance to Heaven. The Chipewyans heard it as an augury of death." First Nation legends are full of loons acting as messengers, so I don't doubt that a loon warned Rickie of the coming hurricane.

Eskimo Curlew: Like the Passenger Pidgeon, the Eskimo Curlew used to exist in breathtaking numbers, but they were shot to extinction or close extinction in the early 20th century. Sporadic reports of them have been recorded since then, but the last confirmed "sighting" was a curlew shot at a men's club in the Barbados in the 1960s. The Eskimo Curlew, like the Ivory-billed Woodpecker is one of the Holy Grails of birding.

Heath Hen: Unlike the Carbonated Swamp Warbler, the previous existence of the Heath Hen is well documented. This bird was related to the Greater Prairie Chicken (Pinnated Grouse) of the tallgrass prairie of the Great Plains. Like the Heath Hen before it, politics and greed are currently pushing the Greater Prairie Chicken toward extinction. The Heath Hen used to be common in New England, but short-sighted management eliminated it on the mainland. Its last well-documented refuge was on Martha's Vineyard (until 1932), but I did find a reference to Heath Hens on a nearby island in Genio Scott's *Fishing in America* so maybe they are still on The Island.

Hen and Chickens: This is a well-know, and feared, reef at the entrance to Buzzards Bay just southwest of Cape Cod.

The Island: I cannot disclose exact location of The Island, but there plenty of islands off the coasts of New England and Long Island that would be a good match.

Leyden Jar: Rickie's firefly jar would have glowed like the antique electrical/capacitor apparatus called a Leyden Jar. It's invention was long credited to Pieter van Musschenbroek, the physics professor at University of Leiden, in the Netherlands.

Montaup Hill: This promontory is currently known as Mount Hope which overlooks Narragansett Bay. Here the Wampanoag sachem Metacomet ("King Philip") sat, and held meetings. He is thought to have used this location to organize his resistance to European settlers.

Mole Crabs: Ever feel something squirmy under your toes when walking the beach? You will probably be feeling these small (1/4 to one inch) crustaceans. Mole crabs bury themselves in the sand in the backwash of the waves at the beach, leaving their eyes and antennae above the surface. Run your hand through the sand of a retreating wave, and you are sure to catch a few. They do not bite or pinch but are amazingly squirmy as they try to burrow back into the sand. I can only imagine what they would feel like inside a bathing suit!

Nanda Devi: Probably most beautiful mountain in the Himalayas and the most tragic, which is saying a lot considering the pathos filled history of this range (Extended Edition).

Nosy Moon: When the nosy moon rises during the meteor watching party to see what the excitement is about, its light washes out the show. In physics, this is called the observer effect; the observation changes the thing observed, but I prefer a simple analogy: It reminds me of trying to look at snowflakes under the microscope at elementary school. An even better example from my youth was the miraculous disappearance of the monster under my bed when the light was turned on.

Orpheus: Originally Orpheus was the god of music, poetry, and prophesy in Greek mythology, but as Baroness Raquel Toad told me, her mother, Rickie, referred to Orpheus because on the these lines from Shakespeare: "Orpheus with his lute made trees,… To his music plants and flowers ever sprung"

Order of the Occult Hand: A silly, secret, and now exposed, message between newspaper writers (Extended Edition).

Phalarope: A lovely shorebird known for twirling and spinning as they pick small invertebrates out of the water.

John Wesley Powell's Right Hand Man: Mr. Toad never understood why this tall tale of his created such an uproar whenever he repeated it at The Inn or why the older members egged him on to repeat it. The reason is that Powell lost his right arm in the Civil War which make Powell's accomplishments all the more remarkable and Toad's story all the more ridiculous.

Red Cedars and the Algonquians: The Native American belief on this subject that is cited by Mr. Toad to his son when motoring through Woods Hole appears to be from an Algonquin tribe known as the Mesquakie (Meskwaki). "Speaking Algonquian language, the Fox tribe of Native Americans, also known as the Mesquakie (Meskwaki), believed that the spirits of their ancestors lived in trees such as cedar and the trees' murmuring in the wind was the ancestors' voices." (http://www.ancientpages.com/2018/01/06/cedar-sacred-tree-medicine-power-native-american-beliefs/)

Saint Elmo's Fire: This weather phenomonon is most often seen on the surface of the ocean as glowing balls, presaging a lightning strike. Saint Elmo's Fire gets it's name from the Italian Saint Erasmus, the patron saint of sailors. The illustrator of this book had a personal experience with the land version of this natural phenomonon during her childhood. This might explain her frizzy hair and sparkling art work.

Storm Surge and Reverse Storm Surge: A hurricane is so strong and its central atmospheric pressure so low that it creates a mound of water that it pushes before it as it approaches a coastline. Most of the damage caused by a hurricane is from the storms surge. Oddly enough, the reverse can happen just before a hurricane hits; the water recedes and the ocean bottom is exposed; Phil Schwind writes of just such an occurrence (before Hurricane Carol) in his book *Cape Cod Fisherman*. This only rarely happens, but it happened to Schwind and our little friends along the Riverside. I should note that any time the tide is unnaturally low, you should be very, very wary because this also happens before a tsunami.

Washerwoman: In a remarkable example of parallel evolution, our New World Mr. Toad also disguised himself as a washerwoman to escape the calaboose. This would explain why the fishing reef called The Washerwoman was Mr. Toad's favorite, and his fishing partners would often comment that he would get all puffed up with conceit when fishing there.

132

Water Ouzel and John Muir: The Water Ouzel is a perky bird of high mountain streams that has a long bubbly song. It was a source of inspiration for John Muir. Interestingly enough, the Water Ouzel can walk underwater. Muir founded the Sierra Club and was instrumental in getting Teddy Roosevelt to designate Yosemite as a national park.

Glossary

Ease off a Point or So: This term is widely used in the Riverside community, even today, but it was first uttered by Long John Silver in *Treasure Island* when he suggested that his pirates needed to, "ease off a point or so on the rum." This book was much admired by the Riverside children, but asking them to ease off a point or two had about as much effect on them as it did on Silver's band of renegades.

Glossary: The veracity of a glossary in a book as whimiscal as this is indeed doubtful, but this particular section deviates a bit from the theme of the book and wanders dangerously close to the actual truth.

Jabroni: This is a term commonly heard along the waterfront to denote someone who is obnoxious, reckless, and/or inconsiderate. Jabronis are common on the fishing grounds, and it is thought that fish breaking on the surface instantly turn respectable animals into Jabronis. As far as I can tell, this word has a Portuguese derivation; the Italian version is the "Jamoke". Whatever its derivation, the consensus is that Jabroni is a fine word that perfectly describes so many fishermen. This term has, alas, recently been adopted by professional wrestlers, which clouds its illustrious maritime pedigree.

Kerberos: In Greek Mythology, Kerberos was the guardian of the underworld, but in this historical context, it is the name of a particularly dangerous reef. Such reefs are sometimes nicknamed the Widow Maker, and there are plenty of them off the coast. At various times the following Widow Makers have tried to kill me: the Sheeps' Pen off Sachuest Point, Cutty Wow Rocks, the Can Opener in Robinson's Hole, Canipiset Channel at Cuttyhunk, and the mouth of the Westport River (multiple times). The most dangerous reef I know of is the West Island breaker off Sakonnet Point in Little Compton, Rhode Island. This has claimed two boats and one life that I know of. It nearly got me one morning when fishing with Mr. Fox.

Turbo-Encabulator: The fabulous turbo-encabulator was first described by a British graduate student named John Hellins and formally published in 1944. This classic piece of techno-babble was made famous by Bud Haggart; it is well worth watching his straight-faced video on YouTube in which he carefully explains the technical details of this wondrous device.

 Interview

In researching the book, I had the great honor of visiting Toad Hall and interviewing Mr. Toad's granddaughter, the Baroness Raquel Toad. Below is a transcript of this historically significant interview.

Q: If you have the time, I have a few simple questions I would like to ask you about the history of your family.

A: Do I have your solemn promise that what I am about to tell you will not be published?

Q: Of course. I am a journalist; I can be trusted.

Q: Did Mr. Toad stick to his claim about discovering the canals of Mars? After Toad and Lowell's "discovery" of the canals, Edwin Hubble (with the 100-inch telescope on Mt Wilson) and others took photographs of Mars and did not find any canals. How do you reconcile this with Mr. Toad's account of the canals on Mars?

A: I am surprised that you would ask such a question; the answer is obvious: climate change on Mars. The canals had dried up by the time Hubble took his photographs. You're not one of those climate deniers are you?

Q: Did your mother, Rickie, ever get to visit the Heath Hens?

A: Oh yes, many times and sometimes she took me....oops I should not have told you that. The very existence of the Hens is a secret.

Q: Would you care to tell us where the hens are?

A: Even if you were a proper animal, I could not tell you that. But you are, unfortunately, human, and as far as I can tell, not the best specimen of that species, so I definitely cannot tell you. Can you assure me that you will not mention the Heath Hens in your book?

Q: Mums the word.

Q: Mr. Toad claimed to have met Roald Amundsen at the South Pole with a warm cup of tea. From what I have read, Amundsen was fanatical about making sure that he had a clear claim to the South Pole after the controversy about who got to the North Pole first. What can you tell me about that incident?

A: My grandfather told me he had to apologize to Amundsen because the tea was warm, not hot. It was brisk that day at the pole.

Q: But scholars all agree that Amundsen was the first to the South Pole; there can be no denying that.

A: Amundsen may have been the first *human* to the South Pole, but Mr. Toad was, thankfully, not human.

Q: What can you tell me about the secret Order of the Occult Hand?

A: Nothing! You are the supposed journalist; you tell me.

Q: Is it true that roasted Mole Crabs were served at your parents wedding?

A: You are going to snicker at this, but Mole Crabs are an important part of our family history.

Q: I see that there are only small pieces of The Canoe still left. Can you tell me what happened to The Canoe? I heard a rumor that its demise almost caused your mother to call off the engagement.

A: Well, my father, Toady, took it out one night without telling my mother.... Well...That's all I want to discuss about this incident. I must say that this interview is making me uncomfortable.

Q: After Mr. Toad spent a night in a pit trap with a couple of skunks, how long did he smell? Days? Months? Years?

A: This interview is over. I think it is time for you to leave. My butler, Tobe, will show you the door.

Acknowledgements

This book would never have been written but for the encouragement of Robert Cocroft, the clever Mr. Rat himself, and my editor at the Providence Journal. Robert was a gentle guide for my various writing endeavors and helped me successfully navigate the shoals while writing the first draft of this book.

I would like to thank my wife, Amy for making the final edits to the text, doing the illustrations and designing this book.

Eve Lesses helped me piece together Mr. Rat's *Lightning Jitterbug* from the sketchy notes that still exist. She also helped me find my sea legs on the dance floor, which is quite difficult for someone with webbed feet. I would also like to thank Sophronia Camp for coaching the dancers when we performed the first *Lightning Jitterbug*.

I am indebted to my editor, Rowan Kream, for providing a fresh perspective and helping to modernized my antiquated prose. But I am sorry Rowan, I had to keep the obscure birds and old epigraphs.

I wish to acknowledge the many colorful characters of Woods Hole in the Old Days who introduced me to the magic of the islands when I was but a cabin boy on my long journey to maturity. Jim Mayvor and I had many discussions about Native American stone artifacts, geomancy, and he even showed me some potential astronomical alignments on Naushon Island. Frank Mather took me on many fishing trips and discussed fisheries conservation with me. I am also indebted to John Buck for long discussions about fireflies at his Wood Hole home. Dan Clark warmed us up with hot buttered rums and nautical stories after our frigid November fishing trips. Most of all I am indebted to the late Gordon H. Browne of Woods Hole (via Marion Massachusetts, and Tangier, Morocco). Gordon and I spent countless days on his boat, the *Mummichog* (the most unseaworthy boat in the history of Woods Hole), fishing and exploring the islands. He told me many tall tales, all of which turned out to be true, and pointed out Pine Island, saying that he remembered when it had cedar trees and dry land. He also told me about a picnic he had on the islands in which they dug up a skeleton at Quick's Hole; it had boots held together with wooden pegs, suggesting to my young, impressionable mind, pirates! Gordon was always an inspiration to me right up until the final trip I took with him on the *Mummichog*, to spread his ashes on his favorite reef, Devil's Foot.

Jenny O'Neill, director of the Westport Historical Society, helped me research the '38 Hurricane. I am also indebted to the staff of the Westport Free Public Library for helping me with my book searches.

Of great help to me during my larval stage was the best fisherman that ever sailed the coast and my tutor on the water, Francis Sargent. In his youth, Fran had actually fished with Mr. Fox, and he taught me Fox's tricks and deceptions. Fran also introduced me to the local Kerberos near West Island off Sakonnet Point, and for years we played cat & mouse with this guardian of the underworld until one rough morning when it filled the boat with green seawater and almost claimed another couple of victims. Also I would like to thank Fran for allowing me to stay in his "Bach" (cabin) on Lake Taupo in New Zealand while I filled out the final form of this book.

Special thanks to Brad Burns for introducing me to John Cole and others of a conservation bent. Brad took me on many wild nocturnal fishing adventures on the dark, windswept shores of Martha's Vineyard and Block Island; may his beloved striped bass be spared the fate of the Heath Hens. Also a tip of the hat to Jimmy White, that fearless and fierce defender of striped bass. During my formative years on the ocean, I am indebted to that famous raconteur Charlie Soares who used to entertain me with his wild stories. Lastly among my fishing friends I must mention Sam Fulcomer who was my companion on countless crazy trips to the islands during the glory days of Striped Bass fishing.

I would also like to thank Michael Silverman, of the Spindle Rock Yacht Club, who took me out in the *Bufflehead* during a solar eclipse and showed me the art & science of sailing a Beetle Cat. Also a tip of the hat to Stuart MacGregor for giving me access to the *Javelin*, a lovely 39 foot Concordia Yawl.

Lauren Miller and Gina Purtell of the Massachusetts Audubon Society were nice enough to show me Allen's Ponds fabulous grasslands so I too could talk to the Bobolinks in one of their few remaining refuges.

I would also like to extend a thanks to Bette Low for proofreading the document.

Major edits to this book were done in the Azores; special thanks go out to Barbara Smith and Edward Dietrich for putting me up in their lovely house in Faial da Terra.

I would also like to thank the owner of the Paquachuck Inn, Brenda Figureido, for the help and encouragement she provided when finishing this book.

This book would never have happened without the help of that old silver expert at the Tilden-Thurber jewelry store, "Uncle" Al Drummond. He gave me a copy *The Wind in the Willows* when I was but a wee lad. I did not appreciate it at the time, but was charmed when I re-read it as a young man. At that point it was too late to thank Uncle Al; this book is my thanks him.

Barbara Walzer deserves thanks for cultivating my writing interests and introducing me to the Peterson guides.

Dr. Alan Poole was especially helpful with my ornithological research. It was he who reminded me to include that very special secret of The Island.

Thanks also to an aptly-named Welcome Swallow at Lake Taupo in New Zealand who would fly in our door each morning, swing around the living room a few times while I was writing, chirp a hello, and exit. I am sure it was looking for a nest site, but it seemed to me that it was urging me to finish this book.

And lastly I cannot possibly fail to acknowledge my little animal friends, without whose help this book would not be possible.

Thanks go out to the current riverfront community. They graciously granted me unprecedented access to their records and spent many afternoons discussing their memories of that fateful summer.

Special thanks go out to Mr. Toad's granddaughter, Baroness Raquel R. Toad, for all the time she spent with me going through the family archives and showing me various artifacts such as The Inn's burgee and old Mr. Toad's outfits (including his driving goggles and gauntleted driving gloves). I was awed and delighted when she showed me their most treasured family heirloom, the transom from the *Runabout*, which hangs in the study of Toad Hall today. It was quite a thrill to see a part of this legendary craft that was so instrumental in the history of The River with its original varnished brightwork, its bronze lettering, and even some ruddy copper paint below the waterline. To think that it was Mr. Toad's son Toady himself that applied (under duress) that paint was awe inspiring.

I am indebted to the Badger clan, Haggis McBadger in particular, for inviting me to dine with him on the lovingly restored Concordia and finding the scavenger hunt riddles. Thankfully he also provided the answers to the riddles for I could never have figured them out on my own.

Thanks also go out to Mr. Rat's grandson, Royalston, for showing me Rickie's journal and sketchpad. Without these, this book would not have been possible. Unfortunately The Canoe no longer exists, but I was thrilled when Royal showed me a thwart from it that survived and still bore a small, inconspicuous T engraved on it by Toady himself. I was also delighted to see the birch bark Catamount etching that has been framed and now hangs in Toad Hall. It was interesting to read the clippings from *The Times* that the family had preserved of the dust-up between Mr. Rat and the birders of the fusty British Ornithologists' Union. Royal also showed me the surviving lyrics to the "Lightning Jiggerbug". I was thrilled to see that it was in his grandfather's hand, with additions by Rickie. Sadly, the Whip-poor-will stanza is still missing and presumed lost to history. I invite readers to try their hand at this stanza and send me what they come up with.

Thanks also to the Mole family for recounting that fateful day when Mr. Mole and Mr. Rat were almost caught by the terrible cataclysm that devastated the community.

I am indebted to the local constabulary for granting me permission to interview Crassus "Sticky Fingers" Weasel III who is serving time in the Hoosgow for some creative accounting when he was Town Treasurer.

And lastly I would like to thank my six-legged friends, especially the persistent firefly who clung to my screen almost every night during my convalescence. This little friend challenged me to decode his dots and dashes. Also the crickets and katydids who would serenade me after dark, lull me to sleep, and most certainly communicate with my dream state. I do hope this book will inspire you to keep your windows open on warm summer nights and listen to their story, which is as compelling as anything I could possibly write.

In the Wake of the Willows

Frederick Gorham Thurber

About the Author

Frederick Thurber earned a BA degree from Brown University. After moving to Westport, Massachusetts he wrote about the wildlife of the Southcoast for over 20 years through his weekly column, "Woods & Waters" in the *Dartmouth Chronicle* and *Westport Shorelines*. He has also been a guest nature columnist in the *Providence Journal*, and produced an audio version of his nature essays for Rhode Island Public Radio.

Thurber began his writing career during the Striped Bass collapse of the 1980's where he was a passionate advocate, and voice for their conservation.

His discoveries with Geoff Dennis regarding the foraging habits of the Hermit Thrush have been published in a technical birding (ornithological) journal *The Wilson Bulletin*.

This is his first book.

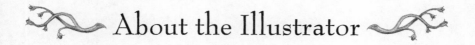

About the Illustrator

Amy Thurber grew up in the woods of Central Connecticut, where her father taught her geology, ecology, fishing and the wisdom of the woodland creatures, trees, and wildflowers. After earning a BFA degree in Illustration from Rhode Island School of Design, she moved to Little Compton, Rhode Island, and then Westport, Massachusetts.

Her illustrations and graphic design have appeared in local publications, and with her husband's nature columns. She has also dabbled in farming, and now grows unusual plants to create her leaf pottery.

She currently resides in South Dartmouth, Massachusetts, with her husband, son, pet cat, pet dove, and 10 beloved hens.

147

CPSIA information can be obtained
at www.ICGtesting.com
Printed in the USA
BVHW030145100719
553024BV00003B/9/P